Secrets of the Dead

An Ambrose Lincoln Novel

by Caleb Pirtle III

Produced by Venture Galleries LLC
1220 Chateau lane
Hideaway, Texas 75771
214-564-1493

ISBN: 978-1-937569-58-7

*Never in the field
of human conflict
was so much
owed by so many
to so few.*

–Winston Churchill

1.

EVEN THE LATE October sky wore black to her funeral. The gathering storm clouds hung like a flannel shroud above the graveyard, ominous and foreboding, not unlike the face of the stranger who stood ramrod straight just behind a mound of red clay that would forever remove the young woman from her place on earth.

His eyes, as hard as cracked marble, never left Ambrose Lincoln.

Lincoln dismissed him with a glance.

But he burned the man's image deep into his brain. He didn't know why. But he wanted to remember the man even if he never saw the stranger again. Not quite six feet tall. Square chiseled face. Pencil mustache. Sloped shoulders. A scar that could easily be mistaken for a half moon carved just below his left ear. A nervous right eye, or was it just lazy? A suit as black as the sky. Perfectly tailored. A raincoat to match. If the man had a gun, it was well hidden. Lincoln had no idea why he even thought that the stranger might be carrying a gun.

He heard the minister quote the twenty-third Psalm.

Something about the valley of the shadow of death.

It sounded familiar.

Ambrose Lincoln promptly forgot it.

He looked again at the wooden rosewood coffin placed gingerly on the rails of a metal bier. It had been opened. A brusque wind ruffled the dark hair of his wife.

She no longer cared.

It no longer mattered.

He heard a woman softly cry.

She had hugged his neck. She said she was his mother.

A tall man wearing a gray suit that would have been new in 1929 and probably worn less than a half dozen times since, lay a hand on Lincoln's shoulder. The man had the crude, powerful grip of a steel worker. He said he was Lincoln's father.

Ambrose Lincoln forced himself to look again into the face of the one who had been his wife.

So young.

So pale.

So soft.

So dead.

He hoped she had died quickly. He hoped she had not experienced pain. He hoped that her final breath had been as easy to take as the first breath of a sleeping child.

He had no idea how she died.

No one had told him.

He hadn't asked.

Ambrose Lincoln had been parked on the eighth floor of the Adolphus Hotel in downtown Dallas when the phone rang.

It was sixteen minutes past midnight.

He wasn't asleep.

He picked up the phone and listened.

That's what he had been taught.

Don't talk.

Listen.

He waited.

"Ambrose Lincoln?"

"It is."

"Your flight leaves in two hours and forty-two minutes."

"Airline?"

"United."

He didn't ask where he was going.

Ambrose Lincoln never asked where.

His ticket would tell him.

That would be soon enough.

"It's your wife," the voice said.

Nothing.

Lincoln kept waiting.

"She's dead."

"The funeral?"

"Tomorrow."

Lincoln broke his own code.

"Is that where I'm going?" he asked.

"It is."

"Home?"

"Memphis."

The phone went dead.

Ambrose Lincoln had heard the voice before.

Harsh.

And brittle.

Somewhere in the distant past.

Then again, it may not have been so distant.

The flight to Memphis had taken less than three hours, even with the angry turbulence of December slamming against the propellers. It was still dark when the plane touched down. Lincoln took a taxi to the Peabody Hotel, grabbed three hours of sleep, emptied two cups of straight, hot coffee down his throat, and walked out to wait for the limousine, as black as the day had broken.

He had not called for the limousine.

He knew it would be there.

It always was.

The church had been virtually empty, just a preacher, a corpse, a grieving family, a husband who had yet to shed a tear, and a stranger – solemn, stoic, and obviously out of place. They had all walked to the small graveyard on the eastern side of the church and waited for the preacher to deliver his final words.

With any luck, Lincoln thought, the good brother would say *amen* before the rain began. He hoped there wouldn't be any singing. There wasn't.

Ambrose Lincoln looked once more and for the last time into the face of his wife. His eyes glanced from his mother to his father. She was wiping away tears with a white lace handkerchief, and he was standing strong and straight, his arms folded in defiance, his jaws clenched. They were family.

They were his family.

He could not remember ever seeing any of them before in his life.

The face of his wife was no more familiar than a face in a second-hand magazine.

Instinctively, Lincoln turned his head slightly to find the stranger, the man in black. Thunder rolled across the land. Lightning danced atop the gnarled limbs of an ancient oak.

The stranger was gone.

Maybe he had never been there at all.

2.

HERSCHEL GRYNSZPAN HAD sat far into the night, staring at the bent postcard that lay before him on a small wooden table in the darkened corner of Le Perroquet. He had not moved for half an hour and appeared to anyone who glanced his way to be in a trance or perhaps already dead, or simply dead drunk. All blood had drained from his face. His eyes were pale, and Herschel had loosened his drab gray and red striped tie in order to breathe more easily. His white shirt was as wrinkled as the postcard, and he had worn a dark woolen suit to beat away the cold winds that were cutting down the narrow streets of Paris. With a trembling forefinger, he began to trace a broken outline around the hand-scrawled words. A tear had dried just below his left eye.

Herschel Grynszpan was only seventeen, far too young, the grumpy, pie-faced waiter knew, to be sipping red wine in a cabaret where the gypsies came in from the raw winter woodlands to play their own brand of jazz. But the young man no doubt had money. The wine was expensive. His tips were always much larger than a waiter would normally expect to receive, and, by the fourth glass, the boy was being treated as though he was much older. The wad of francs in his pocket had bought him two decades worth of age. The waiter smiled and filled his glass for a fifth time.

The walls around them echoed with the sounds of drunken, often boisterous, laughter and the jazz of guitarist Dijango Reinhardt. The light flickered in the lamp beside Herschel, but he ignored it.

The message on the postcard was short.

His sister had obviously written it on the run.

He had tucked her words to memory in case the postcard was lost or destroyed, and surely it would be, maybe even before morning.

The French did not bother him. They were well tailored men, beautiful women in velvet gowns, laughing together, dancing together, falling in love before daybreak, and leaving without ever learning each other's names.

Inside, the world was warm and safe.

Just beyond the door, the innocent were dying.

Some were already dead.

They just didn't yet know it.

But Herschel knew.

He wished he didn't.

He remained motionless but cut his eyes toward a German officer standing at the bar, a black boot propped up on the tarnished brass foot railing. His shoulders were square, his jaws clenched, his right hand resting on the butt of a revolver in a holster made from black leather. His gaze shifted from table to table, from face to face. The officer with an SS patch on his uniform had walked in an hour earlier. He was yet to order a drink. He simply stood there watching. Always watching. His eyes burned like a poker left too long in the fire.

Herschel Grynszpan could feel the German's gaze cut him to the quick. He turned away and kept his face veiled by the shadows.

He barely dared to take a shallow breath.

He knew his face might be his death warrant.

From birth, he had looked exactly like the person he was. Not even age, a French haircut, a new home, and a new identity could mask the fact that he was a Polish Jew.

Corrine Gauthier sat down beside him before Herschel was even aware she had walked into the cabaret. She was still wearing the plain black straight skirt and white blouse of a barmaid. Her thick brown hair dropped to her shoulders and held her face, he knew, the way his hands should be holding it.

She smiled, then frowned.

"What's wrong?" Corrine asked. Her voice was edged with concern.

"They're gone," he said.

"What happened?"

"They're dead," he said.

Corrine glanced down at the postcard beneath Herschel's fingertips. His hands were trembling. His face was drawn and as pale as his eyes.

"The postcard?"

He nodded.

"Can I read it?" she asked.

He did not answer.

For a moment, Herschel Grynszpan was silent.

His eyes moved from the postcard to the German officer and back to the postcard again.

"It's from my sister Berta," he said.

Corrine waited.

"She says the Germans have my family," he said.

"Why?"

"We are Jewish."

"I didn't know."

He shrugged and expected Corrine to immediately stand and walk away.

She didn't.

"My family left Poland years ago," he said, "and went to Germany. My father built his business there. It was home. We thought it would always be home. The Germans came a week ago and took them."

Corrine frowned, deeper this time, and brushed back a tear. "What did your sister tell you," she asked. Her voice was quiet, barely above a whisper.

Herschel shrugged and handed her the postcard.

She read: *They took us in police trucks, in prisoners' lorries, about twenty men in each truck, and they took us to the railway station. The streets were full of people shouting, 'Jews out, out to Palestine.' No one told us this was going to be the end. We haven't a penny. Could you send us something?*

Corrine suddenly found it hard to swallow. She looked back at Herschel, who was staring at the red, baroque wall, his back turned to the German officer.

"What will they do?" she asked.

"They're dead," he said.

"Do you know for sure?"

"I can feel it. When a Jew dies, we all feel it."

"Maybe you are just frightened." Corrine paused, then asked, "Can you send them something?"

"Where?"

"Surely you can find out where they have gone."

"If I ask, the Germans will take me, too."

"But this is France."

Herschel shrugged. "The Germans are everywhere."

"France won't let them take you."

"France won't care."

The German officer had left the bar and was making his way through the crowd toward Corrine and Herschel Grynszpan.

Herschel pulled the collar of his coat up higher around his face. He looked at Corrine and took a deep breath. The splinters of shadow and light had wrapped themselves like ribbons around her.

"Do you know where I can get a gun?" he asked.

"You don't want a gun," she said.

Herschel smiled for the first time.

"Somebody," he said, "is going to die."

3.

AMBROSE LINCOLN KNEW all about inquisitions. Some good. Some bad. Most of them bad. And a few of them deadly. This one, if the phone call made sense, and few of them did, was little more than a therapy session. Somebody wanted to dig down inside his mind and re-connect the cobwebs that dangled loosely somewhere within the fractured seams of his brain.

He walked into a vacant office, tossed his rain-streaked jacket across the back of a sofa and settled down in a black leather chair. He had not slept since the funeral of his wife. He had caught a plane back to Dallas as soon as a private flight could be chartered out of Memphis, as soon as the first cold, wet clod of dirt had been thrown on an unknown grave.

He closed his eyes and remembered the soft contour of her face.

She was beautiful, even in death.

He wished he had known her.

He wished he knew anybody.

Then again, maybe it was better that he didn't.

Lincoln did not have to look around to know he was alone. He would remain that way for four minutes and twelve seconds. It was a game that psychologists liked to play. Treat him like a rat in a dark maze. Test his patience. Then pounce like a jungle cat out of the darkness. Catch him off guard and count the threads in his frazzled nerves. Leave him alone. Let him stew for a few minutes. See if anxiety untangled those frazzled nerves and left the raw ends exposed.

Lincoln smiled.

It was, he had decided a long time ago, a game that fools played. He closed his eyes and let his mind drift away. He had no idea where it went, but it was somewhere on the far side of worry and pain. Ambrose Lincoln spent a lot of time in a place as black as night when the world was devoid of stars, and the moon lay behind a thunderhead that kept the storms away.

It was a place of death, and he wondered why so many feared it, and he could not figure out why he fought so hard to keep from tumbling into a black hole that felt as cool as the stones of a tomb and smelled like the freshly-turned earth of a new grave.

The psychologist was right on time, which meant she was four minutes and twelve seconds late.

This woman walked briskly into the room, removed her gray woolen coat, draped it across the chair behind the desk, and immediately dimmed the harsh glare of an overhead light with a simple switch on the wall. Ambrose Lincoln knew she was armed. He knew where to look. He also knew that she would die, if anyone wanted her dead, before she had time to remove the small Beretta Tomcat from her garter belt, probably brown to match her suit.

The black widow had arrived, and he remained motionless in the web. His eyes narrowed, and his muscles tensed, and he had no idea why. Lincoln watched her every move from the overstuffed black leather chair where he had been waiting for the past four minutes and twelve seconds.

He didn't glance at his watch.

He kept the time in his head.

An old trick.

A learned behavior.

He had forgotten who taught him.

But he still remembered the voice, harsh and brittle.

She was probably too tall and certainly too heavy for three-inch heels. She wore them with the grace of a disgruntled army officer coming down the hallway in hobnailed boots. She didn't walk. She marched, her square shoulders erect, her big hands clutching the black leather briefcase as tightly as if it were a nightstick.

The suit had faint patterns, outlined in black, and looked like gabardine. Her dark hair was cropped short and woven with a few strands of gray. She may have washed and combed it that morning. Then again, maybe not. Lincoln guessed that, in all probability, she had slept alone.

She stared at him from behind thin, wire-frame glasses, which gave her the look of judicial authority. She wore little makeup, if any at all, and no lipstick. Her face was as bland as her eyes, the color of ash long after the embers had ceased to burn. In another time, in another place, in another dress, bathed in a dimmer light, she may have been a striking woman, Lincoln thought. But the drab, loose-fitting suit hid what traces of femininity she might have had. Her cold, piercing eyes removed the rest.

She smiled when she saw him.

Lincoln doubted it was genuine.

"Good afternoon," she said methodically and without warmth as she placed the heavily scarred briefcase on an oak desk, opened it, and removed a thin leather-bound notebook with a pen attached. "I'm Dr. Gretchen Sloane."

Lincoln nodded.

From somewhere behind the credenza came the faint sounds of a classical piano, muffled by the darkness, played as if Beethoven had stopped off in a New Orleans bar on his way to the grave. The piano was ready to cry or break out in laughter at any minute. The piano just couldn't make up its mind.

Lincoln had read somewhere that only a thin line separated genius from insanity.

The same line stood between a man's emotions.

Good.

Or bad.

Ambrose Lincoln no longer crossed the line.

He stayed on his side.

He just didn't know which side it was on.

4.

DR. GRETCHEN SLOANE leaned forward and placed her hands on the desk, palms down. She was precise. She was proper. Ambrose Lincoln had never seen her before, but she would, no doubt, work him over like a surgeon at an autopsy table. Their eyes met. Hers burned. His looked past her.

Ambrose Lincoln had already seen her soul.

"I guess you know why you're here," Dr. Sloane said.

Lincoln nodded again. "They tell me you can crawl inside a man's head and dig out his secrets," he said, his voice barely audible. A wry grin gently creased his face. It was the look of a man who had been judged, condemned, and no longer gave a damn.

"Is that what you want me to do?" she asked.

Lincoln shrugged. "You're the doctor," he said. "I'm here because I've been told you can sort through the nightmares and make a few of them go away."

"Are you worried about the nightmares, Mr. Lincoln?"

"I prefer to call them gentle reminders."

"Of what?"

"That's what you're supposed to find out," he said.

"The nightmares can be erased only if you sincerely want them erased," responded Dr. Sloane.

"You have thirty minutes." His voice was dull, flat, defiant.

"No." She smiled again. "We have the rest of your life," she said.

Dr. Gretchen Sloane removed her glasses and waited for him to respond. Lincoln remained silent.

His face was the worn slate gray of a weathered tombstone with a thin scar below his hairline and a larger one still ragged on his throat. His eyes were empty. The lights had gone out. Then again, his eyes were cutting into her like a surgeon's scalpel.

Once, they may have been blue.

The blue had turned deep purple.

Then black, as scarred as her briefcase.

She waited for him to blink.

He didn't.

Dr. Sloane made her own mental notes that she would file away in her notebook as soon as the session with the curious Ambrose Lincoln ended. She crossed her legs and stared hard at him. He appeared, for all the world, like a man whose soul had left him even though the last flickers of a pulse stayed behind.

His hair was brown, but the flecks of gray had left it as ashen as lava spilling out into a sun burnt desert. It had been carelessly combed, probably dried by the wind, moistened by the rain, and he needed a haircut. He looked to be somewhere between his early thirties and mid-forties. It was difficult to tell. The years had not been kind to him. His face was pale, his cheeks sallow. He had broad shoulders and hands scarred even worse than his face. When he spoke, his words were as direct as a fatal pistol shot.

His nerves were taut.

She saw it in his face. She had seen the same body language once in a large timber rattler that was coiled and waiting to strike.

Only Lincoln was different.

He would give no warning.

Dr. Gretchen Sloane was a practicing psychologist, trained to diagnose and assess mental disorders and emotional traumas endured by her patients. Her job was not to cure them but simply judge whether or not they were still functional in a civilized society. She had studied under the best and brightest professors at Stanford and Yale. Those who worked with her often described Gretchen Sloane as brilliant, and she now possessed a short list of impressive clients.

Only one of them mattered.

Her office on the twenty-eighth floor of an old red brick building overlooking downtown Dallas was only temporary. It had white, sterile walls with no pictures, shelves with no books, a desk without a phone. It smelled of fresh paint. The leather chairs carried a hint of dust.

She rented by the day.

This time, she needed only one.

Tomorrow, she, her notes, and her diagnosis would be gone.

If all went well with Ambrose Lincoln, she would be gone for good. Of course, it all depended on him.

What did he remember?

What did he know?

Could he be trusted?

Was he still a weapon?

Or, as those at the brokerage house liked to say, was he still responsive? Had he already died? Should she simply put his mind at rest and bury him for good?

"Let's start from the beginning," Dr. Sloane said.

The wry grin flickered on his face only for an instant, then vanished altogether. The shadow fell back in place. He wore khaki trousers that had lost their crease a long time ago, a brown dress jacket, still wet from the rain and thrown over a black sweater, and well-scarred boots fashioned from cowhide.

"Most stories have a beginning," he said. "Mine doesn't."

5.

THE MUSIC DIED away in Le Perroquet. Dijango Reinhardt had put away his guitar and was taking a break. He had slipped into a backroom with a bottle of hard liquor and a lady in violet, similar to the color of midnight when the moon was high in the sky. Those who had been listening to him play were on their feet, snapping their fingers, trying to get a waiter's attention, ordering more wine and laughing in quick, harsh bursts of frivolity. The dancers remained where they stood, arm in arm, in love forever, in love for the moment, in love for ten dollars, and ten dollars could buy a lot on the dark side of Paris. A thick veil of cigarette smoke clustered around the chandeliers and hung above the tables like a yellow fog when the wind forgets to blow. It was a good time to leave.

Herschel Grynszpan squeezed Corrine's hand in his, tried to smile, and failed miserably. The German officer had walked past their table, paused a moment with a curious frown, and stared at them, cocking his head and squinting to see them better in the dim light. Corrine forced a smile. It was ignored. Herschel sipped his wine in hopes that the glass would hide at least part of his face.

The German took out a small notebook from his coat pocket, jotted down a few words, nodded to Corrine without a word, and moved on toward the door.

"See," Corrine whispered, "you are safe here."

"He knows."

"You simply fear the Germans."

Herschel glanced down at the postcard on the table. *Did the German see it,* he wondered. *Had he read the words? Did he know about the Jewish families being taken in Hanover, rounded up like animals, sent to God knows where? A jail? A prison? A slaughterhouse? Worse?*

"The German will be back," he said.

"I have friends," Corrine said. "They will protect you."

"No."

Herschel rose to his feet.

"They will hide you."

"They will sell me," he said.

"What makes you say that?"

"When someone is threatened with death," Herschel said, "and he knows it is not his time to die, then he will tell the Germans exactly what they want to know."

"Then you don't know my friends." Her voice had grown angry.

Herschel looked down into the worried face of the girl. She was still holding his hand, refusing to let go. "It's best if I just leave," he said.

"For you?"

"For us all."

"I will never betray you," Corrine said. A tear blemished her face.

"And I will never let them take you," Herschel said. "If I am gone, they will not bother you."

"Where will you go?" she asked.

"Someone has to die," he said. Herschel had said it once. He said it again. He turned and walked away, leaving Corrine struggling for words.

"I will never see you again?" she whispered.

Only her ears heard.

Herschel Grynszpan had walked into the night.

It was as though he had crawled into a grave and pulled the dirt down on top of him.

Corrine wanted to run after him.

But the German was out there.

Waiting for him.

Waiting for her.

She let him leave alone.

Corrine was not ready to die.

Herschel walked the streets in silence. Behind him, the sounds of laughter grew dim. A black car drove by. A dog barked. An old man was sitting on the stoop of an apartment house, sleeping. An empty bottle of cheap wine had broken on the ground beside him.

Within fifteen minutes, he had slipped down one alley, cut across a street where he never walked, hailed a cab, and ridden to his three-room flat. He had not seen the German again. No one had followed him to the old brick apartment house. He was sure of it. Herschel climbed five flights of stairs, slipped inside a dark room, and locked the door behind him. He was breathing as heavily as if he had run all the way from the cabaret.

Herschel sat down on the edge of the bed.

He did not turn on the lights.

A well-lighted room in the middle of the night might arouse suspicion if the German was waiting down on the street below and looking for him, and surely the German would be, if not tonight, then tomorrow.

He closed his eyes and tried to conjure up images of his sister.

And his mother.

Locked away.

Dying.

Maybe even dead.

Already the images were fading.

It was not yet morning.

The night still lay in the darkness.

And Herschel had not moved, had not slept. The room was quiet and dark. *It must be how a grave must feel*, he thought.

The knock on the door startled him.

He held his breath and did not move.

The knock came again, louder this time.

Herschel stood and eased across the room.

Maybe it would not be the German, he thought. *Maybe it would be Corrine*.

He opened the door and looked into a face he had not expected to see.

The face belonged to Dijango Reinhardt.

"I understand you want a gun," he said.

Herschel nodded. "I can pay for it," the boy said.

Dijango stared at him, his eyes dark and foreboding. He reached out and placed a Hungarian M37 pistol in his hand."

"What does it cost?" Herschel said.

"If you use it to kill a German," Dijango said, "the pistol has no cost."

Herschel heard the footsteps walking toward the staircase, but by the time he looked up, Dijango was out of sight and gone.

Herschel held the pistol to his chest.

He had never fired one before.

He hoped, with a certain amount of desperation, that he would be able to pull the trigger when the time came, and he knew that time was growing short.

6.

THE PAST DID not concern Ambrose Lincoln. It belonged to the dead, and they were waiting for him, and he wondered how many of them were dead because he had walked into their midst. He had dreams sometimes, but they, little more than flashes of color and distant sounds of prayers, screams, and a casket lid being closed in the night. The memories of a prison can do that for a man.

"Did you ask to see me?" Dr. Gretchen Sloane broke the silence. She might as well. She knew that silence was a place where Lincoln had dwelled for a long time.

"No," he said.

"Did anyone order you to see me?"

"I was asked to be here."

"Then you have no objections?"

"I have to be somewhere."

Dr. Sloane glanced down at her notes. She was silent for a moment, then said, "Tell me your name."

"It's been misplaced."

"Your business card says that it's Ambrose Lincoln."

"My business card says a lot of things that aren't true."

"I'm curious," Dr. Sloane said, her eyes brooding, maybe even foreboding. "Where did you acquire the name Ambrose Lincoln?"

"In Ratibor."

"Germany?"

He shrugged. "Poland claims it," Lincoln said.

"A soldier?"

"No."

"What were you doing in Ratibor?

"What does anyone do in Ratibor?"

"You tell me."

"Trying to get out."

"Were you there on business?"

"I had my choice between hell and Ratibor," he said. "Apparently I made the wrong choice."

"How many years ago?"

"I try not to remember."

"Why not?"

"I'm the artist."

"What do you mean?"

"I'm the man who draws blanks."

Dr. Sloane stood up, walked around to the side the desk, sat down, tilted her head slightly, and asked softly, "What do you remember, Mr. Lincoln?"

He closed his eyes and tried to scrape his way past the pile of salvage scrap metal that had buried his distant past. Or was it last week. Time was the great illusion. Now you see it. Now you don't. Now you have it. Now it's gone. "I know it was winter," he said at last. "It was cold. The snow had been falling for weeks. It was night. The whole city was dark. No lights. No moon. Nothing. Just darkness."

"What were you doing in the cold?"

Through the faint haze that had been draped across his memory like a piece of surgical gauze, Lincoln again saw himself walking through the snow. The cold had not seared its way to his bones.

"I had gone to meet a man," he said.

"Business?"

"I was being paid."

"By whom?"

"The mailman." Lincoln grinned. "He brought the checks."

All of his yesterdays had become as empty as the narrow and ancient street that stretched far beyond his gaze.

His mind was as pitch black as the night that had swallowed him in a cold, deadly mist.

Dr. Sloane asked again, "Then what happened to you?"

"I woke up in a prison cell."

"Why?" she asked.

"Wrong place," he said. "Wrong time. Wrong town."

"Were you tried in court?" Dr. Sloane asked.

"No."

"Who convicted you?"

"There were two of us in the alley," Lincoln said. "He had a gun. I didn't."

"What were you convicted of?"

Lincoln shrugged. "Wrong place," he said again. "Wrong time. Wrong town."

"Were you injured?" Dr. Sloane asked.

"I healed."

The bullet wound had not killed him.

He ignored it.

He kept the details to himself.

"What was the fight about?" Dr. Sloane wanted to know.

"I had something he wanted." Lincoln smiled sadly. "It was something he wasn't supposed to have. He took it."

"What did you have?"

"A box."

"What was in it?"

"I wasn't paid to look in the box," Lincoln said. "I was paid to deliver it."

"Who was supposed to receive it?"

"The man in the newspaper."

"What was he doing in the newspaper."

"Obituary," Lincoln said.

"Was there a fight over the box?"

"If so, I must have lost," Lincoln said.

"Does that bother you?"

'What?"

"Losing."

"It's not something I dwell on."

"What do you dwell on, Mr. Lincoln?"

"Waking up tomorrow in no worse shape than I am today."

For a moment, Dr. Sloane let the silence linger between them. Her brooding eyes met his. She frowned.

He didn't.

She blinked.

He knew she would.

Finally, she asked, "Were you carrying a gun that night?"

"Why would I have a gun?"

"It's just another alley I have to explore."

"A blind alley, I presume."

"You seem to have plenty of those, Mr. Lincoln."

He glanced out the window. The sun had fled behind a cloud, white and spackled with gray, not unlike the snow clouds above Ratibor. But Dallas would have neither ice nor snow, which was just as well. Dallas did not function well in cold weather. "I didn't't have a gun when I woke up," he said.

"I find that a little odd," she said.

"I find it a little odd that you don't already know," he said.

"Why would I?"

"You have my file," he said.

"These are someone else's observations," she said.

"And what were their conclusions?"

"That you are a very disturbed and dangerous man, Mr. Lincoln." His grin was as cold as her eyes.

"Do you agree with that conclusion, Mr. Lincoln?" she asked.

"I agree with everybody," he said. "A man lives longer that way."

"Why do I not believe you?"

Ambrose Lincoln lay his head back against the top of the black leather chair and closed his eyes. "Hardly anybody does," he said.

7.

DR. GRETCHEN SLOANE looked up from her notes, trying hard to read his face. His mind was like a slab of wet concrete. Full of imprints, but none of them made sense. A man's eyes, however, when in the presence of a woman, any woman, always gave him away.

Lincoln's eyes were resting in a quiet repose. There was no color, no flicker of recognition, nothing etched on them. They kept looking past her as though Gretchen Sloane was no longer there. Maybe he had come to the conclusion that he wasn't in the room either. The dark mind of Ambrose Lincoln had simply walked away and never bothered to come back.

It was just as well. Knowledge could condemn him, convict him, and maybe even kill him.

Ambrose Lincoln had his secrets, but they would remain lost and adrift within some twisted corner of a decaying brain that had been shattered in so many pieces that time would never be able to heal them or put them back together again.

Ambrose Lincoln was the Humpty Dumpty man.

The doctor smiled.

A cold smile, Lincoln thought.

A hard face.

Calculating.

And even colder.

"You said you had nightmares," she said.

"I walked to the edge of a pit one night and fell in," Lincoln replied. "I climbed out. Pieces of my memory are still in there."

"Maybe you didn't want to bring it out."

"It's not something I'd throw away," he said.

"There is a strong possibility that your nightmares are simply hiding reality," Dr. Sloane said as she leaned forward and folded her hands atop the desk, "Perhaps you are afraid of reality. Perhaps you don't want to remember what really happened to you, and so you have mentally created a mythical circumstance in a mythical place to keep you from facing the truth. Do you want to know the truth, Mr. Lincoln?"

"Truth for one man is a lie for another," he replied.

There it was again.

The voice.

Harsh.

And brittle.

Who had told him that?

And why?

Dr. Sloane walked to the window and gazed down on the crowded streets of Dallas at dusk. The shadows were long, as slender as the streetlights that cast them. The neon lights were waiting for night. The old corner bar had empty glasses to fill. People were running into hotels and out of them, chasing taxicabs and sending others on their way.

So much chaos.

So much confusion.

So much noise.

She relished the quiet inside the room and behind the tinted glass window. Without turning, she asked softly, "Do you have the time?"

"No."

His voice was suddenly dull and devoid of any life.

"Who does?"

"The man with the ticket."

"When do you leave?"

"When the watch stops."

"Has it stopped?"

"It still ticks."

"What kind of ticket."

"A train."

"Which train?"

"The last one out."

The room darkened.

The lights flickered.

No.

His mind darkened.

His thoughts flickered.

The words had spilled out of his mouth before he knew he had spoken them, and he had no idea why he said them, what they meant, why she had asked him such a foolish question, or why he had even bothered to answer it.

There was no train.

And no ticket.

Not in the snows of Poland.

Or was it Germany?

If there was, the train had left far too soon.

And without him.

The train had forgotten him.

He listened for the ticking of his watch.

He looked down at his scarred hands.

They bore the faint traces of too many stitches.

Most had healed.

For an instant, he thought he saw his hands tremble.

He forgot about the train.

He heard it. There was no mistake.

It was a long, lonesome whistle fading in the distance.

It was the sound of dying.

The watch kept ticking.

He heard it.

But where was it?

He did not own a watch.

Lincoln shut down the ragged edges of his memory and locked it. The darkness vanished as quickly as it had draped his eyes like an executioner's hood

He looked up and said, "You've asked a lot of questions."

"It's what I do?"

"I just have one question to ask you," he said.

Dr. Sloane dropped her notes into the briefcase and closed it. It was difficult to tell whether or not she was looking at him. He saw her shoulders tense. Her face had grown hard again. "Go ahead," she said.

"What are the chances of me being crazy?" he asked.

"Mr. Lincoln," she replied, "in a world gone mad, we are all a little crazy in our own way. We would not be able to survive in this world of chaos and wars and rumors of wars without some measure of insanity to hide behind."

"Do you have nightmares?"

"I don't have time for my own," she said grimly, glancing at her watch and frowning. The afternoon had gotten away from her. Dr. Sloane hurriedly picked up the briefcase and straightened her glasses.

"Is this it?" he asked.

"Until next time." She reached the door, paused before opening it, and turned to face him. "I'll let you know about next time."

He nodded. Nothing out of the ordinary. There would be no next time. Dr. Gretchen Sloane was giving up on him. Almost everyone had done so.

Ambrose Lincoln watched her leave the office and walk hurriedly down the hallway, the sound of hobnail boots echoing against the bare walls of a metallic corridor, her shoulders rigid, her briefcase in hand, her gray woolen coat thrown awkwardly around her shoulders.

She passed the row of elevators and kept walking.

As he left the office, he looked for her name on the door.

It wasn't there.

The room, the hallway, the elevators were as vacant as his mind.

8.

HERSCHEL GRYNSZPAN HAD not slept at all. He lay in the darkness, clutching the M37 pistol, and waited for morning. There was reason to waste his time on sleep, he told himself. He would soon be sleeping for a long, long time. There was little doubt about that in his mind.

Herschel had been a fugitive for months.

In July, the Prefecture of Police in Paris had, with neither remorse nor regret, turned down his request to remain in the country. He was a Polish citizen. He was a Jew. He was no longer wanted in France. Herschel could not stay, nor could he leave. He was trapped within the web of a political and diplomatic war that was strangling his every breath.

Herschel would never be able to go home to Germany. His passport had expired, and, besides, Poland had closed its borders to all Jewish citizens, even those who carried Polish passports and citizenship papers.

He was dangling between two countries.

The border had no lines.

It may as well have had a wall that touched the sky.

And now, from what he had read in day-old newspapers he had rescued from piles of trash, from the ragged scraps of information he had learned while listening to slurred whispers at Le Perroquet, the German Gestapo was marching through Germany, rounding up all Polish Jews and deporting them to God knows where.

Two days ago, the facts of it all had been merely blurred lines of cold, hard type in wrinkled and yellowed newspaper.

Now he felt the pain.

His family had been taken.

He closed his eyes and could see the scene that played like the broken frames of a bad cinema in his mind. His mother was crying. His sister was begging for a chance to go home one last time and retrieve her clothes. His father was walking straight and stoic, his head unbowed as always. Just ahead, the trains were waiting.

Trains to nowhere.

Trains without windows.

Trains that would rob them of their hope and their dignity.

Trains to a grave.

Herschel shuddered and gripped the revolver tightly. It felt awkward in his hands. He had never held one before. The wind pushing through the open window beside his bed possessed the harsh and unforgiving chill of a late autumn. A light, gray mist was spilling into the room. Maybe fog. Maybe the mist from the rain.

He shivered.

Herschel wasn't cold.

His hands were sweating.

He could end it so quickly, he thought. One second was all it would take, One bullet. One gentle squeeze of the trigger.

He would never feel the pain.

And it would all be over.

Herschel smiled.

It would end tomorrow.

He spoke the words aloud.

"It would all end tomorrow."

The morning gradually grew lighter, but there was no sight of the sun. It lay somewhere on the far side of storm clouds that hovered over France like the soiled bedding on the inside of a pauper's coffin.

Herschel sat down, wrote a brief message on a postcard – *With God's help, my dear parents, I could not do otherwise. May God forgive me. The heart bleeds when I heard of your tragedy and that of the twelve thousand Jews. I must protest so that the whole world hears my protest, and that I will do. Forgive me.* He folded the postcard and stuck it in the pocket of his shirt. He placed the revolver in the belt of his pants and threw a worn coat over his shoulders. It would keep out the moisture but not the cold. Cold no longer mattered. He looked around the room one final time, then walked out to meet the rain.

He was carrying three hundred francs.

He only needed two hundred and thirty five of them. The rest of the money, he figured, would go to buy some French police officer's dinner for the rest of the week. Herschel walked two blocks, the chilled rain pounding his face, and stopped at a gun shop on the corner of Rue du Faubourg St. Martin just long enough to buy a box of twenty-five bullets. The cold had numbed his nerves.

The clerk had not asked why he needed the bullets.

Herschel had not told him.

He caught the Metro, rode to the Solferino station, and walked up the stairs, littered with dried wads of gum, cigarettes, and torn newspapers. An old man was sleeping in a dark corner, unaware that a new day had arrived. He may have been like Herschel Grynszpan and didn't care. The time for caring had passed them both by.

Herschel moved with the crowd out onto Rue de Lille.

Faces he had never seen before.

Faces he would never seen again.

Most were on their way to work.

Most would go home again at dark.

Herschel Grynszpan would not be among them.

He pulled the collar of his coat around his face, wrapped his hand around the butt of the revolver, opened the door of the German Embassy, and walked in. He hoped to meet with the Ambassador. He planned to meet with the Ambassador.

But when the receptionist looked up with a cold glare, Herschel simply said, "I would like to see an embassy official."

"Do you have an appointment?"

"No."

"Are you a German citizen?"

"Yes," Herschel lied.

The receptionist looked him over and scowled. His hair was wet and matted, and beads of rain were falling down Herschel's face, rolling down to the shoulders of his woolen coat. Young. Cold.

Emaciated. Dull eyes. Nervous. The receptionist suddenly smiled. Everyone was nervous when walking into Germany's seat of power in France. The young man was no different. He had a right to be nervous.

The receptionist knew she should send the boy away but thought better of it. The day was much too miserable to chase anyone back out into the rain. Simple boy. Simple problem. He would be out quickly enough as it was.

"Follow me," the receptionist said.

Herschel Grynszpan was led into the office of Ernst vom Rath. The junior diplomat pushed aside the papers he was signing and glanced up at the clock on the wall. It was nine forty-five. By the time, the second hand moved to nine forty-six, vom Roth lay crumpled across his desk and dying.

The papers were smeared with his blood.

The boy had shot him five times.

One for his mother.

One for his father.

One for his sister.

One for himself.

And one because he was a Jew and Ernst vom Roth wasn't.

Herschel Gruynszpan looked down on the diplomat who was struggling to maintain some fragile hold over life. "You are a filthy boche," he said.

"Why?" The receptionist gasped. Her face had lost its color. Her shoulders were trembling. She expected to die.

"I am acting in the name of all the persecuted Jews," Herschel said quietly.

He gently placed the M37 pistol on vom Roth's desk, sat down in a straight-backed chair, and waited for the Germans to come and take him away. He heard frantic footsteps running down the hallway.

He braced his shoulders for the shots that would surely come.

The Germans would sacrifice him sooner or later anyway.

9.

DR. GRETCHEN SLOANE did not finish typing her report until night had settled down upon the streets of Dallas. Her shoulders ached. She felt a faint throb in the back of her neck. She glanced outside the window as the first flakes of a newborn snow began to settle gently on the sidewalk.

She studied the form one last time, the one that asked for her diagnosis.

She would give her opinion and nothing else. There was no clinical diagnosis for Ambrose Lincoln. Someone had made sure of it a long time ago.

She picked up a pen and noticed that she had cracked a fingernail, torn, ragged, and biting into the cuticle.

It was late. She was alone. She had no plans for dinner. She would worry about the nail later.

Dr. Sloane slowly and methodically pulled on a pair of black, tightly fitting, lambskin gloves, made exclusively for men. They matched the color of her briefcase. Once out of sight, the cracked fingernail was out of mind.

All she could think about was Ambrose Lincoln, whoever the poor bastard might be or had been. She thought it over once, weighed the consequences, was too weary to debate her opinion, and finally wrote a single word on the form.

Functional.

Lincoln was not unlike the smoldering and forgotten land mines that had been buried so long ago in a ditch on the outskirts of Tannenberg.

He could still explode.

He just didn't know it.

Dr. Sloane sealed the report in a manila envelope, gave it to the concierge in the Baker Hotel for mailing, and walked out into the bitter winds, waiting for a taxi that would carry her to the train station.

She did not bother to check out.

She never did.

A tall young man with a slight scar above his right eye would show up at mid-morning, pay her bill, and clean up any charges she had left behind. Sometimes, they were messy. Sometimes they required a funeral.

He was the illusionist, she said.

He could make men disappear.

Even though the report on Ambrose Lincoln was classified, perhaps even controversial, and most certainly confidential, she chose not to deliver it in person.

Her travels, no matter how circuitous or how careful she might be, could easily be traced and almost always was. But Dr. Sloane was careful not to leave any fingerprints on the envelope or the forms. She provided money for the stamp. The concierge could leave his fingerprints on the stamp.

She made one phone call from her room on the third floor before she departed. She heard three rings.

Then came a man's voice.

The words were clipped.

The tone was metallic.

"Is he still with us?" the man said.

"He is."

"Does he know it?"

"No."

"Does it matter?"

"When a man is dead, he no longer fears dying."

"Is that an opinion?"

"We deal in opinions."

"I prefer facts."

Dr. Sloane thought for a moment, then paraphrased Lincoln. "Facts to one man are a lie to another."

She heard a short burst of laughter.

Harsh.

And brittle.

"He remembers," said the voice.

"Very little."

"What if his memory comes back to him?"

"It won't," Dr. Sloane said.

"What makes you so certain?"

"He doesn't want to remember."

"But what if it does?"

"Then he will kill one of us," she said.

"He has more reason to kill you than me."

"He doesn't know that."

"He will." The voice said.

Dr. Sloane started to hang up the phone, but the voice asked, "Does he understand the importance of his train ride?"

"He will when it's time."

"What makes you so certain?"

"His memory is gone, not his curiosity."

"Are you sure he is still programmed?"

"For the moment."

"But for how long?

"Longer than he will live, no doubt."

The driver pulled his yellow taxi to the curb, and Dr. Gretchen Sloane climbed into the backseat. She spoke only two words: "Union Depot."

She glanced at her ticket. By this time tomorrow, she would be in Chicago.

Unless Ambrose Lincoln figured it out.

Unless she was dead.

The driver was humming the chorus of *Begin the Beguine*. He nodded and cut away from the tall buildings as sleet began to mix with the snow. Commerce Street was empty, and the lights of Dallas began to fade in the mist around her.

Dr. Gretchen Sloane took a deep breath and closed her eyes. She was not concerned. Not now, anyway.

The lights had faded for Ambrose Lincoln a long time ago.

10.

THE TWISTED MAZE of streets that cat-walked their way between decaying buildings of indiscriminate age were empty, and the color of night was already beginning to darken the narrow back alleys inhabited by forgotten strays and drunken old men who smoked cheap tobacco to warm their innards and chewed it to quench their thirsts. They were men without jobs. They were men without money. They would sleep in the train yard with empty bellies unless the soup lines found a way to fill their empty bowls.

The shadows belonged only to the architecture and to nothing or no one else. The wind had grown stronger now, and patches of ice were forming in the gutters at Ambrose Lincoln's feet.

The streets were blurred with occasional headlights that had been fogged by snow and sleet slowly turning into rain. A secretary fought to keep her umbrella upright in the stiff wind as she crossed the street. A Chevy honked. She waved and was the last one on the sidewalk leading away from the hotel district of Dallas.

A distant train whistle caught the night wind.

Lincoln stiffened.

The train was departing

He felt his pockets for a ticket.

He did not have one.

And in the deep recesses of his mind, he heard the voice again.

Harsh.

And brittle.

The train had departed without him.

Why?

Why should he even care?

A cold rain washed the sweat from his forehead. Lincoln's memory, what was left of it, linked his mind to everything going on around him. Nothing escaped him, no matter how insignificant, not even on a winter night in Dallas.

The morgue is filled with men who ignore or overlook things.

There it was again.

Harsh.

And brittle.

He stood and listened intently.

The train was gone.

Or had the train even existed?

Lincoln walked back to the Adolphus Hotel, disdained the elevator, and climbed the back stairway to his room on the eighth floor. He would see no one on the back stairs. He preferred the solitude. Few died when they were alone. Lincoln threw his jacket over the back of a chair, hoped that it would be dry by morning, and sat down on the corner of his bed.

His memory had been torn into strips. He remembered both sides of the gap, but the gap was a black abyss without a bridge, and time kept rearranging itself on the back landscape of his brain. He remembered the young man in a black raincoat lying dead at his feet but had no idea who had killed him or why he had died. Lincoln had shot someone that night, and his head was filled with ragged photographs of the dead, and none of the faces were familiar to him.

Not even his own.

But when was that night? A year ago? Last night? A lifetime ago? Or was it merely one of the nightmares that crept up on him when he could no longer hold back the darkness of sleep.

Lincoln had been in Berlin.

He was a courier.

That much he remembered.

He delivered things.

He had delivered a small package to the embassy.

But which embassy?

It was a business transaction.

That much he had been told.

He had been paid in advance.

But who paid him?

The man in the black raincoat had taken the package, walked two steps in the alley, then turned around and shot him.

Once.

He could still see the spit of flame.

He had never heard the sound of the shot.

Not even now.

The air around Ambrose Lincoln, even on calm days, was always thick with the acrid smell of gun smoke before the nightmares came, and the nightmares were always waiting for him.

He ran hard.

He had not outrun the nightmares.

The smell of gun smoke burned his throat.

His chest hurt.

He thought he had died, too, lying in the snow, clutching a 9 mm handgun. He remembered the weight of the pistol. He had no idea why he had been carrying one. He had no idea what happened to it.

He had no idea.

Period.

He had been close enough to death to smell it, and it smelled like sweat and garlic. Quiet and cold. Dark and peaceful. Especially dark. It was sleep without the dreams, sleep without the nightmares. No pain. No conscience. Nowhere to run and no need to run. That's all death was. Fear of it was no longer necessary.

For months, maybe it was years – he did not remember for sure – Ambrose Lincoln had lived in and on the threshold of darkness. Daylight came and went. He didn't notice. The seasons changed. He did not see the leaves turn from green to copper and finally to rust. His world during those forgotten days or months had gone no farther than the window of a small room in a fashionable brick manor on a remote mountaintop in the Bavarian highlands.

They called it a manor.

It had been a prison.

Lincoln was sure of it.

His bed was a cold slab of stone.

His room was a cell.

Cold.

And wet from the dripping rains.

The narrow window was never opened. He never looked outside.

Most of the wounds healed. One didn't.

A doctor met with him each morning. Calm face. Frustrated voice. An older gentleman. White hair. Pale blue eyes that looked past him and through him but never at him. And it was always a one-sided conversation. Same questions. All probing the ragged fragments of his psyche. What did he know? What was he hiding? What kind of game was he playing? Lincoln did not listen. The doctor seemed far more agitated than he was.

He spoke mostly in German.

Lincoln did not understand German.

The questions were foreign to him.

So were his answers.

And once a week, someone came in the dead of night and dragged him to a room with thick walls where no one could hear him scream. Lincoln was chained to a table, and a metallic helmet was fitted over his face.

A thick, sour, sponge was jammed into his mouth.

And electric currents played among the dark corners of his mind.

He screamed when the darkness came.

He was still screaming when he awoke on the cold slab of stone in his cell. Somewhere deep inside him, Ambrose Lincoln was screaming still.

11.

NO ONE AROUND the table was speaking. All eyes were focused on the little man with a shock of black, unruly hair falling around his forehead. In the dim overhead light, it looked as though his thin mustache had been painted on with a stroke of black paint across his upper lip. His shoulders were sagging, and his gray woolen uniform was streaked with sweat. He was rubbing his temples with the tips of his fingers as he carefully considered the news he had just received.

"Ernst vom Rath is dead," the messenger had said, his words clipped.

Der Fuhrer shifted his gaze across the faces of his war council.

All were solemn.

Eyes were empty.

Faces were rigid.

Not many looked as though they had slept lately.

He made a mental note of it.

Der Fuhrer did not trust men who slept their allotted hours. Wars had never been won by men who slept. He scratched their names on a blank piece of paper in his notebook. They would not be invited to his next meeting, and there would certainly be a next meeting.

They would be on their way to Poland.

Men who slept would be sleeping for a long time.

Graves were full of them.

The messenger had handed a folder to Joseph Goebbels, the minister of propaganda for the Third Reich. He stepped back smartly and stood at attention beside the door.

Everyone had turned toward the man with the pencil thin black mustache and was waiting for der Fuhrer to say something. Der Fuhrer frowned.

What did they want, he wondered, a declaration of war?

When the little man with an unruly shock of black hair finally leaned back in his chair and spoke, all he had to say was, "Who is Ernst vom Rath?"

"A diplomat in the German embassy, mein Fuhrer," said Joseph Goebbels, still working his way through the papers, all of them clipped together inside the leather folder.

"Where?"

"France."

"Paris?'

"Yes, mein Fuhrer.

"How did he die?"

"He was shot, mein Fuhrer."

"Was it Political?"

"It was."

"Was he one of us?"

"The shooter?"

"No. The man who was shot."

"He was, mein Fuhrer."

"Did one of us pull the trigger?"

"No."

"Then who would dare kill one of us?"

A slight grin played its way across the face of Joseph Goebbels. Or was it a smirk.

"A young man."

"From France?"

"From Poland."

"We have no war with Poland."

Goebbels smiled. He could not help himself.

"It was a Jew," he said.

Adolph Hitler stood and walked to a window on the far side of the room. He watched the splinters of darkness thread their way down the streets of Berlin. The sidewalks were bare of any signs of life, either man or beast. Piles of snow had already begun to bank up against the gutter. A police car stopped at the corner, waited a moment, then moved on.

"And where is he now?"

"He is in custody."

"He is alive?"

"He is, mein Fuhrer."

"He should have been shot where he stood," Hitler said, placing his palms against the chilled glass of the window pains to cool them.

Behind him, a fire was raging in a rock fireplace. The thick stone walls of the council room had kept the heat bottled up inside, and it was suffocating. Der Fuhrer felt as though the hair on the back of his neck had been singed.

"It is better that we keep him alive," Goebbels said.

"Why do you say that?"

Joseph Goebbels stood and walked to Hitler's side.

His voice was low when he spoke. A whisper would have been louder. His eyes were dancing.

"You wanted an excuse, mein Fuhrer," Goebbels said.

"For what?"

"To rid Germany of the Jews." Goebbels folded his arms and pressed his forehead against the window. His breath fogged the glass. He stepped back and, with the tip of his forefinger, wrote his initials in the condensation. "Herschel Grynszpan is your excuse," he said.

"What do you propose?"

"Extermination."

"How?"

"We will find a way."

Adolph Hitler stood silent for a moment. Berlin had succumbed to the darkness of the day. He would not.

"What charges will we bring against them?"

"There are assassins among them,' Goebbels.

"And next time they may not just be content to kill a junior diplomat. They might have someone, shall we say, much more powerful in mind."

"I presume you are talking about me?" der Fuhrer asked.

"Would you blame them?" Goebbels said.

"So what is the point of keeping this man you call Herschel Grynszpan alive?"

"Dead, he is a martyr," Goebbels said. "Alive, he is a failure. We will hand out posters with his photograph from one end of Germany to the other, from one end of Europe to the other. Germans and our allies will understand the Jewish threat. The Jews will see his photograph, read his name, and know why they must die."

"When will the solution begin?" Hitler asked.

Joseph Goebbels opened the window, and a chilled wind slapped both men in the face. It was wet with shards of snow.

He removed his cap.

He waved it once above the street.

Then a second time.

In the distance came the distinct crack of three gunshots.

Three.

And no more.

Joseph Goebbels smiled again.

"It has already begun," he said.

12.

AMBROSE LINCOLN HAD thought he was in a hospital.

It felt like a prison.

But how many years ago was he there?

And was he ever really there at all?

Somewhere on the far edge of his mind, he remembered a nurse changing his bandages. He was no longer bleeding, and he was being treated like the sheet on the bad. No better. No worse. Change it. Keep it clean. Sooner or later, it would wear out.

Lincoln was brought his meals three times a day by an elderly lady who never looked at him or spoke to him. He had nothing to say to her.

She was always smiling.

Why?

She obviously knew something he didn't.

She might know why they came to take him in the night and probe the inner recesses of his brain with electric currents.

A man could only be electrocuted so many times and live.

But how many? And had he reached the limit?

He should ask her. The thought crossed his mind every time the elderly lady placed his tray on a metal table beside the cold stone slab bed.

He never did.

Ambrose Lincoln did not want to know.

He spent his waking hours chipping away at the block of stone that separated him from those lost and ragged strips of his memory. All he uncovered was one brief and blurred glimpse of himself in the dirty snow of an alleyway in a city he had never seen, in a country where he had never been. He had been lost. No. He was misplaced. Maybe his memory, too, was a lie.

His life had become a repository for a lot of them.

The blood had spilled and was drying in the new snow falling gently on his face. Soldiers, bowed against the winds, fighting against the currents, dragged themselves past him in uneven lines, their eyes as hollow as his. The faces were strange. So were their uniforms. Those who glanced at him did not care that he was dying. The whole world around them was dying, and they were struggling to stay alive. Had he seen them? Or had they simply brought the nightmares that disturbed his sleep when he slept, and he hardly ever did.

The voice would one day tell him that the city had been in Poland.

The voice would not lie.

His were the only words that Lincoln ever heard.

And they were harsh.

And brittle.

The 9 mm automatic in his hand had fired until it was empty.

On odd occasions, he could still see a tall, bald-headed man lying face down in the snow, coughing and gagging on his own blood, cursing in an unknown tongue.

Maybe it was a confession, his last rites.

He was not wearing a black raincoat.

What had happened to the man in the black raincoat?

The man who had collected the package Lincoln delivered on the dark side of a dark town in the dark of the night.

The man who thanked him.

The man who looked like a kindly grandfather.

The man who shot him.

And who else was dying in the snow?

Coughing.

And gagging.

Lincoln assumed he had shot the man.

He had shot somebody.

But why?

Why had Lincoln wanted him dead?

Or did he?

Was it an accident?

Or an execution?

And who, if anyone, had ordered it?

When death comes, unheard and unseen, it collects as many souls as it can, keeps a few, and discards the rest. Lincoln had no idea why death had rejected him on that cold night in a town that had not welcomed him as a stranger and was only a dot on the map.

Was it a nightmare?

Or reality?

Ambrose Lincoln wished to God he knew for sure.

He hoped to God he never found out.

The days passed fitfully in the stone manor. One was no different from the last. Small cell. Cold room. Left over food. A nurse who never spoke. A wound that slowly healed. The questions in German. After a while, Lincoln, no longer bothered with the answers. He simply took one breath after another and lay in the night, waiting for the electric shocks.

He looked forward to them.

They provided his one escape from the cell.

The outside world was nothing more than a dark hallway and a therapy unit on the third floor, dank and musty, smelling of urine and sweat.

But it was outside.

Lincoln stared at the gray wall. No longer did he have any urge to unravel the mystery of his past.

It was dead.

And gone.

The electric currents one night put him to sleep. And he awoke on crisp, clean sheets of the Champs Elysees Plaza Hotel in Paris. He did not remember leaving the prison. Lincoln had no idea who had rescued him.

He watched sunlight falling through an open window.

He closed his eyes.

The light blinded him.

He was not yet ready to climb out of the darkness.

13.

BENJAMIN GRUNER HAD been uneasy all day. He hung the scarred black leather camera case over his shoulder and locked the door to his photographic studio as he always did, promptly at twelve minutes after five. The bitter chill of a November afternoon draped around his shoulders, and he shifted his gaze from one end of the street to the other. For the most part, the quiet resort town of Baden-Baden looked like it always did. Workers were on their way home, and the tired were turning into beer halls where they had quenched their thirsts for years. The young were falling in love. The old were hanging onto the only loves they had, and each day was taking all of them a step closer to the grave.

Benjamin Gruner recognized most of the faces. They belonged to friends, to neighbors, to those who had operated their small shops along the same avenue in the same Jewish section of town for a good part of the last thirty years. There were new faces on the street from time to time, but they usually belonged to those who had come for the healing baths and taken a wrong turn. They were almost always lost and apologetic and laughing to hide their nervousness.

The new faces today troubled him.

None of them were laughing.

No one else on the street had noticed them.

But Benjamin Gruner was a photographer. He had been trained to narrow his focus and see what others did not see. In younger days, it was said that he possessed the eyes of an artist.

Now Benjamin was old and frail, with stooped shoulders and a thick white mustache that matched the color of his hair. His energy was fading, but not his eyes.

He counted six of them congregating out front of the synagogue, huddled together, talking with great animation. They were all dressed with brown shirts. They were all young with belligerent faces. One turned and saw him. The eyes were dark. The eyes were lethal.

Benjamin Gruner shuddered and turned away. He shuffled to the corner of the block and stepped into a small, cramped Austrian *bierhaus*. Karl Kauffman was waiting for him, his head down, his shoulders slumped. If Benjamin hadn't known better, he would have thought that Karl was crying.

"It's not a good time to be a Jew," Karl said softly.

Benjamin shrugged. "It has never been a good time to be a Jew," he said.

"I guess you have heard the rumors," Karl said.

"Do you believe them?"

"I am afraid not to believe them." Karl finally took a long swig from his glass. "A member of the Third Reich has been assassinated," he said. "The party hierarchy in Berlin blames the Jews."

"The Germans always blame the Jews."

"They are going to come and take us away."

"Where?"

"It doesn't matter."

"When?"

"It doesn't matter."

Benjamin slammed his fist on the table. "They will have to kill me first," he said.

"They will, Benjamin," Karl said softly. "They will."

Midnight was still two hours away when the sounds of broken glass startled the quiet, sleeping streets of Baden-Baden. Benjamin eased out of bed and opened the window of his home, perched above his studio.

"What's wrong, papa?'

It was the voice of his daughter. She had thrown an old chenille robe around her shoulders and walked into his bedroom. She was tall, a kindergarten teacher, and her oval, alabaster face was almost hidden by long strands of ebony hair.

"I don't know, Rachel," he said.

It took a moment for his eyes to adjust to the darkness. He could see the brown shirts storming down the street, breaking one store window after the other with wooden clubs. Some were waving flaming torches over their heads. Behind them, the fingers of a fire, already burning hot and out of control, had cut through the roof of the synagogue.

"My God," Benjamin whispered.

It was a prayer.

It was too late to pray.

He pulled on his woolen pants, shoved his feet into a pair of aging, scuffed boots, and grabbed his camera, a Leica screw mount with a fixed lens and rangefinder. He dropped a handful of film in his jacket pocket.

"Where are you going, papa?" Rachel asked.

"We are being attacked," he said.

"Give me time to get dressed."

Benjamin turned abruptly and held his daughter tightly by her shoulders. His voice was stern. His words had the impact of a pistol shot. "Do not leave this room," he said. "Lock the door behind me. Hide beneath the bed. And don't open the door for anyone but me."

A rifle shot ricocheted down the street.

A scream.

A burst of laughter.

Rachel ran to the window and looked down as the brown shirts hurled a concrete block through the window of her father's studio. An old woman ran out her door and down the sidewalk. A second shot, and she fell in a crumpled heap. Her body quivered only once before she died.

"Papa," Rachel yelled, "they are killing us."

Benjamin placed a gentle hand over her mouth. "Do not leave this room," he said again. "Do not make a sound. The darkness will hide you."

"What about tomorrow?"

"Pray for tomorrow," he said.

"But it is not wise for you to go out there."

"I must."

"You have no pistol." Rachel was crying now. "You have no weapon. You have no way to protect yourself."

"I have my camera," Benjamin said. "They may well kill me, but the world will see their faces. The world will know what they did to us tonight."

"I love you, papa," Rachel said.

"Love your faith," Benjamin said. "By morning, it may be all you have left."

The screaming in the street grew louder.

The door had closed behind Benjamin Gruner.

14.

THE DARK STREET outside his photographic studio was littered with splinters of glass, but Benjamin Gruner ignored the broken windows and his own growing fears as he ran to the woman who lay in a heap in front of the bake shop two doors down. He knelt at her side and felt for a pulse.

A sudden noise startled him, and Benjamin glanced up into the face of Samuel Feichtmann opening the door to his shop and stepping out onto the sidewalk. He was squinting as he tried to adjust his glasses. The old man was still dressed in his night shirt, and he looked somewhat addled amidst the sounds of gunshots and glass breaking, and the bursts of maniacal laughter bouncing off the walls around him. "What is happening?" Fechtmann asked.

"The Germans. They have been threatening us for years," Benjamin said.

Fechtmann's eyes widened with a touch of horror as he looked toward the flames erupting from the fallen roof and broken windows of the synagogue.

"It is no longer a threat," Benjamin said.

He was still cradling the woman's head in his lap.

"Who is she?" Samuel asked.

"Poor Mrs. Ashendorf."

Fechtmann leaned down for a better look. The dim glow from a street lamp fell across her face.

"I have known Mrs. Ashendorf for years," he said. "She buys my little cookies. Every Friday, she is in my shop. I know her as Sara."

"She is dead."

Fechtmann stood up and watched three brown shirts running down the street toward them.

"Did they do this?" he asked.

"One of them did. Or one like them did."

The taller of the brown shirts pushed Samuel Fechtmann roughly against the wall of his bake shop, and the old man fell off balance and tumbled to the sidewalk. Blood from a small gash in the back of his head began to spill down his face.

Another, the boy with a white band around his sleeve, grabbed Benjamin's shoulders and jerked him away from the woman's still warm corpse. The harsh glare of a flashlight struck the photographer in the face. "We will take them both, yes?" the boy with the white arm band said.

"No," the taller one answered brusquely as he stepped across Samuel Fechtmann, lying crookedly in the sidewalk. "Our orders are strict. We must obey them as they are written. Herr Heydrich was very explicit in them. He wants only younger men, men who can still work. These are old men. They are worthless."

"Shall we kill them?"

The taller of the brown shirted storm troopers grinned. "There is no need to waste our bullets," he said. "These men are old men. When the food is gone, and the water is poisoned, they will die soon enough."

He kicked Benjamin in the face as he walked away.

Benjamin Gruner pulled himself to his feet, picked up his camera, and paused long enough to capture the swollen and blood-streaked face of Sara Ashendorf on film. Her eyes were still open as though she could not believe she had been shot. She could not believe she had died. A small bullet hole had punctured her throat.

Benjamin turned and hurried down the street.

His breath came in short bursts.

His lungs were begging him to stop.

His anger drove him onward.

He stopped only long enough to raise his Leica and fire.

Glass was breaking.

Fires were burning.

From homes.

From stores.

And the synagogue was cloaked in fire, and the wooden walls that had heard so many prayers and confessions rose up like a grotesque skeleton in the night.

Families were running wildly down the streets.

Men cursing.

Women screaming.

Children crying.

A woman fell.

A man died. His head had been torn apart by the bullet from a brown shirt's rifle.

This had become Benjamin Gruner's world, lit the color of daylight by the mass of flames leaping from one structure to another. By morning, the whole street would be encased with embers and shards of glass.

It had become a frightened world.

A tragic world. A dying world.

In black and white.

The world would one day see the execution of a town.

In black and white.

Benjamin knew he had been shot long before he felt the pain of the bullet burning deep inside his stomach. Blood was seeping into his shirt.

He should stop. He knew it. His legs were weak. A wave of nausea swept over him. He was afraid that he would pass out, but he gritted his teeth and crawled ever so slowly down the sidewalk. The skin on his knuckles lay in torn strips.

Benjamin could not quit.

He was one with the shadows.

The young woman was holding her young daughter's hand when the brown shirt approached her. He leered at her and ripped the buttons off her blouse.

She slapped him. He shot her point black between the eyes.

The child screamed.

She was on her knees crying for her mama to get up, begging for her mama to get back up. She was still crying when the bullet tore into the back of her tiny skull.

Benjamin was sick.

But he had it all.

The film would not lie.

He lay in a back alley and watched twenty Jewish men, maybe more, being paraded down the streets of Baden-Baden by a band of brown shirts, laughing and taunting. The ways of men had become the ways of animals.

They were no longer soldiers.

They were thugs.

Assassins.

No heart.

No soul.

The building beside him was burning. The fire was hot against his face. He could not leave. His vantage point was perfect.

He placed his camera on a barrel for support and shot.

He kept shooting.

A taller brown shirt walked up and grabbed one of the men that had been roped together. Benjamin recognized him. He had seen the brown shirt before.

"Too old," the tall brown shirt said.

He threw the man to the ground and walked over him.

One by one, the brown shirts walked over him.

The last one stopped just long enough to put a bullet in his ear.

One last shot, and the world around Benjamin Gruner began growing darker. He fought the darkness. He cursed the darkness. He refused to fall into the abyss.

It was almost daylight by the time he crawled back to his studio.

Brown shirts were still roaming the streets, breaking everyone and every thing that had not been broken.

His strength was almost gone. His hands had lost their feeling. The pain had died in his stomach. This was the way of death, he knew. Death was right behind him. Benjamin worked his way up the stairs, one step at a time. Rachel was waiting for him on the top of the landing. She fell to her knees and grabbed him. She held him tightly.

His face was nothing more than a mask of dried blood.

Rachel started to speak, but he stopped her.

He thrust three rolls of film in her hand.

"They should all know," he said in a husky whisper. "You must let them all know what they did to us."

Rachel raced down the stairs and paused only once to look back over her shoulder. She knew, beyond her tears, that she would never see her father again.

15.

THE WORDS ON the telephone were definitely spoken by a woman. They were crisp and filled with tension. "The train has arrived."

"Does he know why?"

"No. Not yet."

"He has forty-eight hours."

The voice was harsh.

And brittle.

"He will know when the time is right."

"Can you be sure?"

"He lives in a world where there is no sanity, not here, not home, not anywhere," the woman said. "For him, the whole world is an asylum, and he is he only inmate who can not and does not want to escape."

"Until you give him the key."

The phone line crackled.

For a moment, she thought her call had been disconnected.

"Are you still there?" she asked.

"I am."

"Don't worry," she assured the man on the phone. "The situation is under control."

"Is he under the control?"

"He buys the ticket," the woman said. "He takes the ride. Some people get off. He doesn't. When the train leaves, he will be on board."

"Our man needs to make sure it's quick."

Again.

Harsh.

And brittle.

"Dying never is. It only seems to be."

"He must not fail us."

"He knows what to do. He just doesn't know it yet."

"And if he fails?"

"I remove the ticket."

"It could be his last train."

"We all have one last ride."

She hung up the phone.

The bedroom at the top of her hotel was dark.

The moon had again hid its face, and no light made its way past the curtain. She glanced outside the window as it began to fog over from the warmth of her breath.

A new sleet was falling on top of an old snow.

She touched her face to the glass.

It was cold.

Not unlike the aftermath of death.

She smiled.

Ambrose Lincoln would again be asked to kill a man.

Swift.

And certain.

Tonight he would be given the name.

Tomorrow, she would give him the date.

The time.

And the weapon.

Ambrose Lincoln would ask no questions.

He never did.

Ambrose Lincoln fought his own private war within the shadows of a fragmented memory. He had fought the wars of other men and lost. He was a survivor, perhaps, but a casualty nonetheless.

The phone call had come as it always did, in some ungodly hour that dangled beneath death and morning. It was his grim reminder of the night in hell he had chosen to forget. For so long, he had been living within the parameters of an uneasy peace.

He knew when the train would arrive.

His ticket had been waiting at the Adolphus when he checked out.

It had one name attached.

Klaus Wagner.

Lincoln pushed his way through a crowd of business suits, military uniforms, and cigarette smoke, hurrying down the steps that led toward the Union Depot. He was carrying an overnight bag on his shoulder. It was stuffed with wool trousers and turtleneck sweaters. He wore a long leather jacket to keep the snow off his shoulders. His boots needed a new coat of polish, but then they always did. He braced his back against an angry wind that kept whistling around the corner and violently sweeping trash alongside the tracks.

He boarded the train and entered compartment number thirty-four, shutting the door behind him. It was small. It was confining. It was, he thought, no larger than a casket with a bed and running water. Lincoln dropped his overnight bag on the floor and hung up his jacket. He brushed a pile of gathering snow off the sill and shut the window. The noise outside died away in an instant. He preferred the silence.

The streamliner was twenty-two minutes late by the time it rolled out of the station and headed east toward Washington. There would be three changes in three cities before he arrived but none until morning. The train bore through the night as though it were trapped inside a tunnel that had no light at either end.

Ambrose Lincoln locked the door behind him and tried to keep his balance as he worked his way down the narrow aisle to the dining car. He did not take time to notice the tall, angular gentleman seated alone beside the club car bar as he passed by. His dark suit was rumpled. He had obviously been wearing it for several days. His head was bald and glistened as though it had been oiled in the harsh glare of an overhead lamp. His face was hidden behind the front page of the *New York Times*.

The gentleman in the rumpled suit waited motionless until Lincoln was out of sight before he stood, calmly and methodically folded the newspaper, placed a dollar on the table to cover the cost of his whiskey, and left the club car. He face was thin, his skin pale and almost jaundiced. He wore a pair of imported spectacles that he removed and dropped into his coat pocket. His shoulders were slightly slumped, his hands much too large for his body. They were callused, the hands of a workingman. He looked as out of place in the suit as he did in the luxurious club car of the Union Pacific streamliner. He was no more impressive than a beer stain on the gilded bar.

He picked up a small briefcase and limped quietly down the red-carpeted aisle until he found compartment number thirty-four. The number was barely visible in the dimly lit corridor.

He knelt, opened the case, and took a letter from inside a manila folder. It had been lying beneath a German Heckler & Koch P7 9 mm self-loading automatic pistol. He glanced both ways, made sure he was alone, and slipped the letter beneath the door. He picked up the pistol and placed it in a small holster that dangled from his belt and near the small of his back.

He gingerly brushed the carpet fibers to remove any visible traces connecting him to compartment number thirty-four, then stood, putting most of his weight on his good left leg, and limped noiselessly from one passenger car to another.

He would sleep well that night.

He wondered about Ambrose Lincoln.

Or Klaus Wagner.

Or whoever the poor bastard might be.

16.

THE UNION PACIFIC streamliner was almost a hundred miles out of Dallas by the time Ambrose Lincoln found a corner table in the dining car, sat against the red velvet-lined wall, did not remember why it should be that important for him to keep his back covered, and ordered his usual, a glass of tonic.

No gin.

No vodka.

Just tonic.

Ice.

And tonic.

A drunk is nothing more than a sitting target in the crosshairs. He's too slow to think, too slow to move, too slow to react, too slow to get out of the way of a bullet, but not too slow to die. He doesn't know anyone wants to kill him until he looks for his next breath and can't find it.

The words had been spoken by a voice he knew well.

It was harsh.

And brittle.

But the voice did not belong to a face.

Not one that Ambrose Lincoln could remember.

It was simply words uttered from the darkness.

Lincoln methodically surveyed his surroundings. Twenty-four tables, ninety-six chairs, three chandeliers, two of them antique crystal, one bronze and greatly in need of polish, four waiters, most of them older than sixty, none of them foreign, a single metal door leading to the kitchen, a small chrome-plated bar on the opposite wall, a bartender, a slope-shouldered little man with a square face who sat on a barstool reading a Raymond Chandler detective novel between drink orders. More ice than water. More water than liquor. Keep them sober. Keep them drinking.

A small crowd was beginning to ease its way into the dining car, and Lincoln took a mental photograph of each face, although none, as far as he knew, had any importance for him. It made little difference. He wanted to remember them all. Each line, each wrinkle, each smile, each frown, each quizzical glance was promptly registered and filed away among the tattered remnants of his mind. He slowly picked them out. Two salesmen. A business executive. An aging military man, complete with stars on his shoulder, braid on his hat, and a woman much too young to be his wife drinking a dry martini beside him.

A pair of ladies sat in the opposite corner, playing Gin Rummy for a penny a point. Both had gray hair, lace scarves around their necks, and they laughed a lot. The more they drank, the more they laughed. There was one railroad official and either a doctor, a preacher, or maybe a lawyer sitting at a separate table. It was difficult to detect one from the other. The arrogance was all the same.

Lincoln's eyes fell on the small, oval face of a young woman, maybe thirty, maybe not, with long raven hair and a beauty mark or a spot of mud under her left eye. She was barely five feet tall and wore a woolen dress the color of the earth. Her skin was pale, translucent, and had not yet been touched by the sun. She was barefoot and carrying a bleached cotton sack.

The small, oval face was pointed his way, and her eyes were dark, filled with bitterness and regret. They would speak long before she ever said a word. She stood and swayed awkwardly with the movement of the train as she walked toward him.

Lincoln tried to look away.

He couldn't.

The dark, bitter eyes were hypnotic.

Any sign of life had dimmed behind them a long time ago.

"They are lying," she said suddenly.

Her voice was soft and distant.

"Who are lying?"

"The ones who were there."

Lincoln nodded.

"And the ones who weren't," she said.

She sat down at the table and folded her hands on top of the white linen cloth. They were small, fragile, and scarred. Her nails were torn. Her fingers had been bleeding. Lincoln looked closer. It was a spot of mud beneath her eye.

"Where are you talking about?" Lincoln asked.

"My country," she said. "Their country. It belongs to us all. It belongs to no one."

"What are they lying about?"

"The night of broken glass," she said.

Lincoln waited.

In the distance he could hear the mournful whistle of the train, and he saw a few scattered lights from a small town outside the window. The lights flew past, nothing more than a patchwork of flickering glares in the shadows, and then it was dark again.

"They will tell you that the windows were broken, that the streets were lined with splinters of glass, that drunken thugs attacked us. But the thugs are gone is what they will tell you, and life goes on as it always has."

"Who will tell me this?"

"Your newspapers," she said. "Your politicians. Your President."

"Why?"

"The war has begun. They run from the war."

"Which war?"

"My war." The trace of a sad smile touched her lips. "Soon it will be your war."

Lincoln shrugged. "My war has never ended," he said.

She reached out with her fingers and gently touched his hand. Her voice had become a fading whisper. "They broke our glass," she said. "They broke our hearts. They burned our homes. They burned our little shops."

She paused.

Lincoln waited.

"They killed us all," she said. "They killed the old. They killed the sick. They killed a mother. They killed a child. They left them in the gutter to bleed."

"How do you know?" Lincoln said.

The woman stood and walked toward the door.

"I was the mother," she said.

Ambrose Lincoln frowned. His eyes caught a glimpse of the bleached cotton sack she had left on the table.

He stood to catch her before she could leave the dining car.

She was gone.

It was as though she had never been in the car at all.

Lincoln opened the sack and found an envelope. The letter inside had a name.

Rachel Gruner.

Nothing else.

No address.

No phone number.

Just a name.

The envelope had something else inside.

A bullet.

It looked like a 9 mm.

Small and deadly.

Lincoln instinctively knew he had held one before.

He had no idea where or when.

It didn't take a lot of guesswork to know why.

17.

RACHEL GRUNER HAD slipped down the stairs, cloaked in darkness, and waited beside the cracked window, watching the brown shirts take what was left of her little neighborhood and break it with their bare hands.

She heard the screams.

The laughter.

The gunshots.

Someone was begging for a husband.

Someone was crying for her child.

The streets of Baden-Baden were littered with broken glass, burning embers, and the dead.

Rachel walked quickly into her father's studio and picked up a pair of scissors that he had used for years to cut the frames from his filmstrips. She could almost feel his hands when she touched them.

But his hands would be cold by now.

He no longer dreaded morning.

Death had come and walked with him away from the terror and the pain that gripped the Jewish commercial center of the Austrian community. Rachel could no longer run to him for safety. She must leave him for the jackals, the men in brown shirts, the animals who found sport in shooting down old men who could no longer run.

She clutched the five cans of 35 mm film tightly and said a simple prayer before dropping them in the pocket of her Navy woolen coat.

Her prayer echoed the final words her father had given her: Please let everyone know, she whispered silently. *Please let everyone know that they are killing us. Forgive me of my sins, for I will sin before morning. Forgive me for what I must do for I will do it. Now and forever. Amen.*

The brown shirts had passed by.

They were dragging an old man and his son.

The old man fell to his knees.

The tall one shot him once.

Rachel watched them drag the son away.

They left the old man where he lay.

He was singing.

And old song.

Rachel wondered if God had heard.

He would be pleased.

It was the song of Abraham.

And she wondered if God had heard any of the screams that rose up from Baden-Baden, and if he had, why had he not come down and protected them all? Why had he forsaken them?

Only the sinner is punished.

Rachel had believed it all of her life.

So, who among them had sinned?

And why must they all pay for the transgressions of one condemned soul?

The old man was still singing as Rachel Gruner ran from shadow to shadow, passing the bake shop, the flower market, and darting down a black alley. The air around her was thick with the pungent smell of burning buildings. The roof atop the synagogue had fallen, and ash fell upon her face and hair, mixed with snowflakes. The hot with the cold. She ignored them both.

Down the street behind her, Rachel heard a gunshot.

Only one.

And the song ended.

The screams were dying away.

The crying was nothing more than the wind.

The old men were cowering in the darkness.

The young men were marching, their heads bowed, shivering as the snow touched their faces, trembling as the guns pushed them on.

Rachel had no idea where they were being taken.

Neither did they.

In the far distance, she heard the lonely wail of a train whistle, and she knew. The young men would never come home again.

Their mothers would wait.

Their wives would shed tears.

The young men would die long before anyone knew.

Rachel didn't know why.

She didn't know where.

She didn't know why she knew.

But their lives were like the song.

They were ending.

Rachel stepped around a corner and looked up into the face of a young man wearing a brown shirt.

He was not yet twenty, she thought.

He must still be in school.

He carried a black Luger, and it was pointed at her face.

A wicked grin played across his face. He held his hand out to her. "I will help you," he said. "I will save you."

Rachel's face turned rigid.

"You will not go with the rest," he said. "You are young enough to work. You appear strong enough to work. But I won't send you away. I have better things for you to do."

"Why are you doing this to us?" she asked. There was neither sadness nor hatred in her voice. It possessed no emotion at all.

"Your people are like bugs on the sidewalk," he said, a sneer on his face.

"We step on bugs. You should not have gotten beneath our boots."

The brown shirt reached out and jerked Rachel to him. He stuck the Luger in his belt and kissed her roughly on the lips. His breath smelled of stale garlic and hot German beer. He laughed.

He held her tightly.

He tore at her coat.

He ripped the buttons off her dress.

His teeth sank into the soft skin above her breasts.

His breath was coming in short, frantic bursts.

He did not feel the scissors until Rachel had jammed them into his stomach, just above the belt.

Then the pain came.

He tried to scream, but no sound came from his throat.

He stared at her a moment, then dropped to his knees, frantically clawing his stomach, his hands drenched with blood, trying desperately to close the ragged hole beneath his brown shirt.

He was far too busy trying to save himself, trying to live, to see the reflection of moonlight upon the scissors when Rachel shoved them deep into his throat. His body jerked once. He was dead before it could jerk again.

Rachel picked up the Luger and dropped it into her coat pocket and walked away into the night.

She left the scissors with the brown shirt.

That was for papa, she told herself. *It was not enough.*

18.

AMBROSE LINCOLN STEPPED down from the Union Pacific's Overland Flyer while an uneasy dusk was settling across the rooftops and domes of Washington's distant business district. A cold, biting wind stung his face. He buttoned his topcoat, leaned into the gusts of snow, and walked through the lost and confused masses fighting their way into and out of the train station. Everyone was in a hurry. Most of them were late.

Lincoln walked briskly toward the taxi that he knew would be waiting for him. Same color. Black. Same license plate. It would end with the numbers six and two. If he knew the numbers, he wondered, how many others knew them as well? He paused and glanced over his shoulder, searching for a glimpse of the woman in a drab earth-colored dress with a spot of mud beneath her eye. He did not see her, but he had seen her once, and he could not forget the dark hollow eyes that went with her soft and hollow voice.

In his coat pocket, Lincoln carried the German Heckler & Koch P7 9 mm self-loading automatic pistol that had been waiting in his room, lying beneath the pillow with a folder that held his papers and credentials.

He knew where to look. They knew he knew where to look.

Ambrose Lincoln had no idea who left it.

He never did.

He had no idea what he was supposed to do in Washington.

He never did.

He did not know if he was the hunter.

Or the prey.

The voice never told him.

The voice that was harsh.

And brittle.

But Lincoln would know when the time came.

He always did.

He unfolded his ticket and glanced at it again as he climbed into the back seat of the taxi. He did not need to tell the driver where he was headed.

The driver knew.

He had a ticket that said his name was Klaus Wagner.

He had a passport that said he name was Klaus Wagner.

He had a driver's license that said his name was Klaus Wagner.

The message was clear.

It always was.

If something went wrong, they would not bury Ambrose Lincoln.

They would bury Klaus Wagner.

A German.

Maybe a Jew.

He didn't know.

But Ambrose Lincoln, the name, if that was his name, and the man, would simply slide off the face of the earth.

Perhaps he already had.

The taxi pulled into the portico of the St. Regis Hotel. The driver stopped, but his motor was still running.

Ambrose Lincoln handed him a ten-dollar bill.

"It's not necessary," the driver said.

Lincoln dropped it on the front seat and walked away without looking back. The driver had been extremely nervous on his way to the St. Regis.

There was no reason for him to be nervous anymore.

His job was over.

The merchandise had been delivered.

The merchandise had been delivered unbroken.

The driver could go home and get drunk and probably would.

Lincoln checked in as Klaus Wagner and asked if he had any messages. He had one. It had two words written in pencil.

Fitzgerald.

Bar.

There was nothing cryptic about either one.

"Do you have any luggage?" the clerk asked.

"Just what I have on my shoulder," Lincoln said.

When a man lives from one day to the next, he has no reason to prepare for the day after. It was only a promissory note, a number on a calendar, a moment in time that might or might not ever come.

Lincoln dropped his key in his coat pocket, and it nestled beside the German Heckler & Koch P7 9 mm self-loading automatic pistol. He would probably need them both only once. A man had no reason to prepare for a future when he didn't have one.

Lincoln walked straight to the bar.

He hadn't slept in two nights.

Another night wouldn't make any difference.

The room was dark and metallic. A single chandelier hung from the ceiling, above the bar. The bartender was leaning against the counter, his back to the gin bottles, and his arms were folded. A waitress in a long black gown, probably satin, was moving from table to table. She had long, raven hair and a smile for everyone. Everyone had a tip and a burning desire for her. She was a professional, Lincoln thought. She would go home alone with a purse full of tips and retire her smile for the night. She probably hated the smile as badly as he did the pistol in his pocket.

He glanced from face to face.

They were businessmen. They had suffered through another hard day. Some had won. Most had lost. Thus far, they had beaten the Depression. They had jobs. Good jobs. Only men with good jobs came to the St. Regis. They no doubt worked for the government. It seemed that everyone in Washington, D. C., did.

Only one face was staring back at him.

Only one man was expecting someone.

Everyone else had come with a friend, or friends, or was drinking alone. It must be Fitzgerald.

It wasn't the first time Ambrose Lincoln had seen a corpse. But this one was different. This one was still breathing. Only the eyes were dead, sunk back into the hollows of their sockets and glazed over as though they had been varnished with a film of sour milk. The man's breath came in short, labored, and shallow bursts, and each one seemed to be the last.

Ambrose Lincoln had seen it all before.

Only the names had changed.

And the circumstances.

A man's soul died long before his heart was ready to give up.

19.

AMBROSE LINCOLN LOOKED down into the twisted little face
of George Fitzgerald, who had turned away and was staring at an
empty glass that still carried the faint odor of Scotch, the expensive
kind. He was watching the last shards of ice melt away. His gray suit,
with dark, thin stripes, was a little too crumpled, his white shirt a
little too wrinkled, and his red silk power tie hung loosely around
his neck, devoid of any power.

He was slightly built with sagging shoulders and a thick mop of
unruly brown hair that obviously defied either comb or brush. The
man's face was gaunt, his eyes were magnified a little too large
beneath glasses encased with fragile black rims, and he appeared as
emaciated as a prisoner staggering out after a month's worth of
solitary confinement.

George Fitzgerald had watched every step Lincoln made as he
sauntered past the bar, stopped just long enough to order a tonic –
no ice – and then ambled with purpose toward him. From a distant
corner, a neon jukebox crooned the music of Glenn Miller in case
someone wanted to dance. No one did.

When Ambrose Lincoln reached the table, there was no greeting,
friendly or otherwise, and no need for one.

Neither man had ever met.

Nor did they need to be introduced.

George Fitzgerald held his breath.

The man in the Navy woolen coat had arrived to replace him.

Or kill him.

He never knew which, and the uncertainty of it all was fraying his nerves. He was tired of being afraid.

George Fitzgerald had known about the ominous specter of Ambrose Lincoln for as long as he had worked as an attorney and liaison for a company that chose to operate out of the basement of an abandoned building on Eighteenth Street, three blocks from the White House. No phone calls came into or out of the offices. No one had a business card or a title or a rank. There was no name on the door. No one ever came in. All business was conducted elsewhere, and no one ever talked about what he did. Sometimes, far more often than anyone wanted, a new face would show up, and a prayer would be said for the old face. Nothing more.

All Ambrose Lincoln remembered, when he remembered anything at all, was that, for some godforsaken reason, the streets and deserts were piled with bodies when he walked out of a place. The good fell with the bad, and Lincoln seldom realized there was any difference between the two. He lumped those around him in two categories: the living and the dead. He had not yet decided in which category he belonged. The jury was still out. The jury had been out for a long time.

George Fitzgerald represented the new face of the company. He was bright. He had finished near the top of his class in Vanderbilt Law School. He could have gone to work with any major law firm in the South and made a lot more money, but George gave it all up to work in the dimly lit and musty rooms of an abandoned building, where decisions were made that the government wanted but never sanctioned. His father said it was a mistake. His law professors said it was a mistake. His wife said it was a mistake. It was a mistake.

Ambrose Lincoln knew this about George Fitzgerald but had forgotten why he knew. George in less than five years had followed too many rabbit trails to too many dead ends, going by train, or plane if necessary, from one distant corner of the country to the other, from one god forsaken patch of a disturbed world to the next one, and they were all disturbed, from one back-alley brothel in Amsterdam to the next run-down police station on the edge of Moscow, crowded with the flotsam of life, from one execution which he had refused to watch to a secret safe house whose cover had been blown by a front-page, above-the-fold story treading dangerously on treason and closer to libel. He left the final tattered remnants of his nerves alongside a railroad track on the German border with Poland.

Lincoln drained his glass of tonic and sat down at George's table.

He had no idea why he was in Washington.

He figured he would know before morning.

He always did.

He looked hard at George Fitzgerald. "My name is Ambrose Lincoln," he said in a calm, reverent voice that was no more audible than a whisper.

"I know who you are," George said.

"Do you know why I'm here?"

"You're here," George said, "because Robert Priestly isn't."

"And where is Priestly?"

"Do you know him?"

"No."

"This was his job," George said. "I just made the arrangements."

"What was his job?"

"I don't know."

"What arrangements did you make?"

"A plane ticket," George said.

"Where?"

"Austria."

"So why am I here?" Lincoln asked.

"I can't reach Priestly," George said. He looked down and sucked on a dry glass. "They sent you."

"Want another Scotch?"

"I'm quitting."

"Is Priestly lost or merely misplaced?" Lincoln wanted to know.

"It might be worse."

"Is he still in town?"

"I have no idea," George said. "He and I had an early dinner a week ago last Monday. Said he had a meeting that night with his source. He caught a cab outside about nine-thirty. I haven't seen him since."

"Is that unusual?"

"Not for Priestly." George shrugged. "He's on time even if the clock isn't."

"You got a name?" Lincoln asked.

"For what?"

"His source."

"Nobody knows his sources." George laughed softly. "He comes and goes, and if he's still alive when it's all over, I guess he's won."

"Got any idea where we can start looking for Priestly?"

"Too late."

"For Priestly?"

"For me." He removed a sealed envelope from beneath his empty glass of Scotch and shoved it across the table to Lincoln. "You can give this to the man for me. It's my resignation."

"You know the way to his office," Lincoln said. "I don't go there."

"Maybe not," George said, "but I'd rather they find the resignation on your body than mine."

20.

GEORGE FITZGERALD HAD drunk too often and far too long from a cauldron boiling over with lies and rumors and rumors of lies. But reality had replaced the idealistic dream of a young attorney who thought he could change the wrongs of a world beset by far too many wrongs.

His had been a hard lesson, and now he had begun hearing footsteps behind him. No faces. Just footsteps. Most of his negotiations took place between angry, bitter men who preferred to barter with a .38 caliber pistol. George went by the book until he realized there was no book.

Ambrose Lincoln looked at the resignation George had handed him. "The man doesn't like assets who quit," he said.

"I've been offered another job." George smiled for the first time. "It's a big firm in Memphis," he said. "Good benefits. The pay's a lot better."

"I'm sure the hours are no better.."

"I'm tired of it all," George said. "I had a wife. She's gone. I had two kids. They're gone. I had a good name. It's gone. I'm not even sure I know how to practice law anymore."

George Fitzgerald glanced up, and Lincoln saw his face for the first time. The dim overhead light made a dark purple bruise lying beneath his left eye even darker. George's cheek was crusted with dried blood. The blood had smeared his white shirt collar like a prostitute's lipstick. Too red and too moist. His lip was swollen.

Ambrose Lincoln smiled softly. "You're afraid this time, aren't you?"

"Priestly was in over his head."

"What's he dealing with?"

George shrugged.

'Said it went all the way to the White House if his sources weren't lying to him."

"Sources always lie."

"I got a phone call," George said. "Man said he had a message for Priestly."

"Who?"

"The man that hit me."

"You go to meet him?"

George nodded.

"Armed?"

George shook his head. "I'm an arranger," he said.

"I've heard they wanted to kill me for years," Lincoln said.

"I believed him."

Lincoln nodded. "Then it's a good time to quit," he said. "When you're afraid to go to sleep and troubled about waking up, it's time to move on." Lincoln finished his tonic and signaled for another. "You going into criminal law?" he asked.

"Civil."

"Lawsuits?"

"Divorces."

"Maybe you'll get your wife back," Lincoln said.

"Maybe." George shrugged." She thought I was unstable," he said.

Lincoln nodded again. "Familiar ground," he said. "I've lived there for years."

George stood and tried miserably, without any success, to straighten the wrinkles from his suit. He look one last sip from an empty glass – a force of habit – and reached for his wallet.

"I'll get the tab," Lincoln said. "You go wash the blood off your face."

"I've had several."

"The man can pay for several."

George Fitzgerald turned to leave, then stopped and looked around. "I have a folder that Priestly mailed to himself," he said. "He wasn't in. He hasn't been in. The hotel left the folder with me."

"You read it?"

"No."

"Curious?"

"No," George said. "It's up in the room," George said. "I'll bring it down to you on my way out. You and Priestly can figure it out if you find him. I'd just as soon not know what you decide to do."

"Priestly have a room here?"

"Five twenty-six," George said. "It's empty."

Ambrose Lincoln watched him walk out the door, then turned his attention to the waitress walking toward him and carrying his tonic. A little too tall, he thought. Too thin. Too much hair. Too young for a man his age. He shrugged, smiled, and asked for her name anyway. It might be a long week.

"You married?" she asked.

"I can be if it makes you more comfortable," Lincoln said.

"It doesn't."

"Then I'll keep the ring in my pocket."

She laughed and turned away. It was a good, hearty laugh. He liked women who weren't shy about laughing. Then again, he wasn't opposed to shy women who never laughed.

When George Fitzgerald had not returned in twelve minutes and thirty-eight seconds, Ambrose Lincoln downed his tonic, threw a hundred dollar bill on the table, and walked out of the bar. The waitress might not be interested in him, he thought, but the Depression was on. She would damn sure remember him.

Twenty dollars bought him George Fitzgerald's room number from the young lady behind the front desk. She said she wasn't supposed to give out the room number of a paying guest but didn't mind writing it on a notepad if that would work just as well. Lincoln said it would. She waited until he glanced at the number, then quickly wadded up the piece of paper and dropped it in a trash can.

"If you want to call, I can connect you to his room," she said.

"He may have already left," Lincoln said.

He was walking toward the elevator when the door opened.

It wasn't the first time Ambrose Lincoln had seen a corpse. But this one had drawn his last breath. George Fitzgerald lay crumpled in the back corner of the elevator. One arm was draped across a black leather suitcase, his feet were twisted up beneath him, and all blood had drained from his face. The bullet had entered his left eye, just above the dark purple bruise. A snub-nose revolver lay in his lap.

Lincoln shifted his gaze across the elevator floor, looking for a file folder that might contain Robert Priestly's notes, if one did exit. He did not expect to find the folder. He wasn't disappointed.

All he saw was an airline ticket for Memphis neatly stuck in the breast pocket of George's tailored suit. The plane would have one empty seat when it departed Washington. Lincoln knelt and opened the young attorney's left hand, which had been knotted into a fist. Inside he found a torn napkin, and he read the single name that had been hastily scrawled with a pen:

Rachel Gruner.

The ink had smeared the last *r.*

21.

THE SOUND OF boots crunching broken glass outside the basement window startled her, and Rachel Gruner fought her way out of a fitful sleep. The boots always came in the early morning while the random splinters of daylight were spilling with hesitation down the black streets of Baden-Baden.

She curled up beneath the thick-legged butcher's table and held her breath until the footsteps faded, and silence returned to settle down into the darkness again.

Rachel had spent two nights, and this was the second day, in hiding as the band of brown shirts methodically went from house to house, from shop to shop, searching for anyone who had a Jewish name or a Jewish look in their eyes.

She had watched them through a crack in the wall.

She had cried as she watched them through a crack in the wall.

The nightmares did not come when she slept at night.

The nightmares roamed the streets of Baden-Baden.

The nightmares would not end until the Jews were gone.

And the Jews were leaving on their knees.

Women had been raped, again and again, cowering like frightened animals when the predators tracked them into the forests, then they were thrown aside like rag dolls to die, left naked in the freshly fallen snow while their clothes were soaked with kerosene and burned.

Children were beaten.

And brutalized.

They cried out until they realized no one would hear.

Then their cries died away, and the children crawled back into the darkness of their fears, wondering why no one had come to save them, never realizing that the only ones who could save them had been dragged through the town and jammed into the cattle cars of a freight train headed to Poland.

Rachel had watched them go.

Shoulders sagging.

Faces bloodied.

Eyes hollow.

On they walked over broken glass.

The parade of the damned.

The brown shirts were moving from door to door.

German soldiers were herding the prisoners away.

When old men could walk no farther, they were shot.

The fortunate ones were shot.

The young would die a thousand deaths before a bullet brought them mercy.

Rachel could hear the sound of boots coming closer.

The laughter.

The cursing.

She knew it was only a matter of time before they would find her.

She clutched the five cartridge cases of film that her father had given her. *The world must know*, he had said. *Everyone must know what they are doing to us.*

The brown shirts might find her.

They could not find the film.

She might die.

She might be humiliated and dead in the cold streets before another morning came to Baden-Baden.

But the film must survive.

The world must know.

Rachel shook her head to clear the cobwebs from her brain. She was tired, and cowards were born from the womb of exhaustion.

No.

She could not die.

She would not allow herself to die.

The film would survive.

The world would know.

Rachel knew she could not leave the film in the butcher shop. The shop would be burned the way the rest of the homes and stores were being burned around it. The air was thick with the smell of embers in the wind.

She dropped the five cartridges in her coat pocket and picked up a meat cleaver from a cutting board. She might die, she thought. But someone would beat her to hell.

Rachel slipped through the back door and glanced down the alleyway. For the moment, it was empty.

Pressing her body against the back wall, she eased toward the far end of the block where the bakeshop lay in smoldering ruins. Rachel stepped out into the street. In the distance, a siren wailed.

A man shouted.

A gun fired.

Then another.

A woman screamed.

Rachel whirled around and saw the trucks plowing their way past the synagogue, moving steadily forward, taking out anything or anyone who could not escape their wheels.

They squealed to a stop, and armed troops leaped to the ground, fanning out and working their way through the marketplace.

Screams echoed down the street.

Then curses.

An old man, too stubborn to run, or maybe he was simply too tired, stood in front of a truck, his arm raised in open defiance.

A German officer shot him dead, once through the forehead, neatly and quickly and without any sign of remorse.

There was a rifle shot.

The bullet kicked up the cement and dust at her feet.

A man groaned and pitched forward, face down in the dirt.

The screaming had become contagious.

Rachel heard running feet of soldiers growing closer behind her. She did not look back.

She ran.

"Stop!" The command came in German.

Rachel didn't.

She kept running, shoving her way past frightened forms with frightened faces that seemed to be moving in all directions at once and going nowhere. She bolted toward an alley that led behind the hollow hull of a building, still thick with smoke and ash.

"Stop!"

The rifle fired again.

A woman kept screaming, and she wouldn't stop, and it wasn't until Rachel had fallen into the blackened shadows hovering around the walls of a dead building that she realized the screams were coming from her own throat.

22.

THE AMBULANCE HAD beaten the night patrolmen to the St. Regis Hotel, and the ambulance wasn't going anywhere. The interns on board had taken one glance down at the face of George Fitzgerald and knew there was no reason to check his pulse. It had no doubt bled out as well. There was nothing for them to do until the late shift of the District of Columbus Police Department arrived. Wasted days and wasted nights. The crisis docs knew all about them.

The older intern – the one with slicked-back black hair and a clipped mustache – turned to Ambrose Lincoln, leaning casually against the wall.

"You find him?" he asked.

"I did."

"You shut off the elevator?"

"I did."

"Touch anything?"

"Just the switch."

"Don't go anywhere," said the intern. "Police will be here in a minute."

"I wouldn't dare go anywhere." Lincoln said.

"Why not?"

Lincoln grinned. "I like to see the big city boys work," he said.

It was obvious that Detective Sergeant Dudley Stovall was in charge by the way he came swaggering through the front door. His dark blue overcoat was wrinkled and fraying around the collar. But it shut out the wind and kept his Navy blue suit dry from the drizzle that had settled over the aging buildings of downtown Washington.

His square face was chiseled, but years had managed to soften the edge. His glasses were too thick and, and the hotel's heat had fogged them.

Daniel Hofstra trailed him across the lobby. He was a young man with thick and brown hair matted against his head by the rain. He was well over six feet and as thin as the sharp edge of a razor. He had already removed a notebook from his jacket pocket and was searching for a pencil. He wore the solemn frown of a small town undertaker on his way to the burying ground. Ambrose surmised that he was the eyes and ears of the homicide team. Stovall made the decisions. Good or bad. It didn't matter. He made them.

Both detectives knelt beside the little man lying drenched in his own blood. Stovall fished a leather wallet out of the victim's hip pocket. He opened it, frowned, and announced, "Name's George Fitzgerald."

"From Memphis," said Ambrose Lincoln.

Stovall glanced up. He had paid no attention to the big man leaning against the wall with his arms folded. A stranger who knew more about a dead man than he did immediately aroused his suspicion.

"You know this man?" Stovall asked.

"We're acquainted," Lincoln said.

"You known him long?"

"A couple of hours."

"You kill him?"

"Don't carry a gun," Lincoln lied.

"Which means you could have killed him."

"If I had a reason," Lincoln said.

"But you didn't."

"Somebody did."

"Know who it might be?" Stovall asked, standing up and shoving both hands into the pockets of his overcoat. He wiped the residue of the cold rain from his face.

"No," Lincoln said.

"You two gentlemen doing business together?" Stovall asked.

"Not exactly," Lincoln said. "Mister Fitzgerald was an attorney. He had run across some problems on a case he was investigating. I was sent to replace him."

"That make him mad?"

"He offered to resign."

"Was he scared?"

"Not of me, he wasn't."

"Who?"

"He didn't say."

"You an attorney?" Stovall asked.

"No," Lincoln said.

"Then what makes you think you could replace him?"

"He dealt with numbers."

"And you don't?"

"I deal with those people that others don't want to mess with," Ambrose said.

"The bad guys?"

"Sometimes."

"And other times?"

"The real bad guys," Lincoln said.

"These folks Mister Fitzgerald was investigating, what were they involved in?" Stovall wanted to know.

"I have no idea."

"The mob?"

"He didn't say."

"What did he say?"

"That he was resigning."

Stovall shook his head and stuck a wad of day-old chewing gum in his mouth. "We've had a real bad string of bad luck with the mob," he said.

"They ever need attorneys?"

"Who?"

"The mob."

"That's our problem," Stovall said. "They have better attorneys than we do."

Ambrose Lincoln shrugged. "They wouldn't have wanted George," he said.

The coroner walked between the two men and entered the elevator. He was short and stocky, a year or two past his fiftieth birthday, with close-cropped hair that never needed combing. He dropped his medical bag beside the corpse and took time to wipe the rain streaks from his glasses.

"What have I got?" the coroner asked. His voice was coarse. He had obviously been asleep and wasn't too pleased about being awakened. He was never in a hurry. The dead certainly weren't.

"Gunshots," Stovall said.

"How many?"

"I'm gonna let you count 'em all," he said.

"How long has he been this way?" the corner asked.

"Forty-eight minutes and sixteen seconds," Ambrose Lincoln said.

The coroner looked over his shoulder with a hard stare. "Who are you?" she asked.

"He found the body," Stovall said.

"You're pretty damn precise," he said.

"I left Mister Fitzgerald fifty-eight minutes and sixteen seconds ago," Lincoln said. He paused and searched an empty circuit of his brain. "No make that fifty-nine minutes and nine seconds now. He was supposed to be down to meet me in ten minutes. He was right on time."

"With a bullet in his head."

"If you say so, "Lincoln said.

Daniel Hofstra was taking notes. It was what he did best.

"You're a precise sonuvabitch," Gerald Waskom said.

"I get paid by the hour," Lincoln said.

"The coroner glanced down at the crumpled body of George Fitzgerald. "He supposed to be paying you?" she asked.

"He was on his way out of town."

"He'll be delayed a day or two."

Ambrose Lincoln shrugged his broad shoulders. "Mister Fitzgerald was used to delays," he said.

23.

EVEN BEFORE HE opened the door to Robert Priestly's hotel room, Ambrose Lincoln sensed a terrible dread. He didn't know why. He didn't know what caused the sudden apprehension. But he felt like a man who had stepped into a dark alley and heard the quiet, deadly sound of a pistol being cocked. All he could do was wait for the bullet.

Lincoln saw her sitting in the shadows on the far side of the room, really nothing more than a vague silhouette outlined against the dim light of a table lamp.

Same dark hair.

Same wire-rimmed glasses.

Same hard, unemotional eyes.

The suit was black this time, and the thick, padded jacket hung loosely around her broad shoulders.

In her lap lay a Browning 9 mm Luger.

Lincoln knew the make and model of the pistol as soon as he saw it. He didn't recall ever seeing one before.

Did she want to kill him?

No, Lincoln decided.

If she did, he would already be a corpse.

He would be with George Fitzgerald, and the two men would be leaving earth together.

Beneath the pistol lay a manila folder. It had been stained by a smattering of dried blood.

Lincoln knew where she had found it.

Had she killed to get it?

Poor George Fitzgerald.

Dr. Gretchen Sloane saw him glance at the folder.

"He had resigned," she said.

"Did he tell you?"

"No."

"How did you know?" Lincoln asked.

"We are paid to know, you and I," she said.

"He was just a harmless, frightened little man," Lincoln said.

"When a man knows too much, and he leaves," Dr. Sloane said, "he leaves for good."

"That's not in the contract," Lincoln said.

"It's in the fine print," Dr. Sloane said.

"Who reads the fine print?"

Dr. Sloane shrugged. "The man does," she said.

The room suddenly grew colder as though someone had opened the window. Dr. Sloane sat back in the chair. She lifted the pistol and scraped the barrel with a fingernail until a patch of blood was gone. The shadow had removed one side of her face. All he could see were her eyes.

Cold.

Calculating.

The ominous stare of Dr. Gretchen Sloane was hypnotic.

She spoke once.

His eyes flickered like a spent candle.

And the room went dark.

It was as if Ambrose Lincoln, with the snap of her fingers, had gone blind.

He stood erect.

His eyes remained open.

Lincoln might as well have been dead.

The room went from dark to black.

"Has the train departed?" Dr. Sloane asked softly.

"It has."

"Who had the ticket?"

"I did."

"A new train is departing."

"I don't have a ticket."

"It has been issued."

"Not to me."

"You had a passenger. You were not going alone."

Lincoln remained silent.

He waited.

"The passenger's name was Robert Priestly."

Silence.

"Only one of you will leave the station."

He tried to breathe.

"Robert Priestly must be left behind."

There was no air in his lungs.

"He did not return the ticket."

Lincoln's blood was pounding. He could not feel it.

"You cannot leave without it.'"

The chill around him was numbing.

"You must find the ticket."

Dr. Gretchen Sloane stared at Lincoln.

He waited.

His eyes had not yet blinked.

"Do you have any questions?" she asked softly.

"No."

"The train will leave on time," she said.

Lincoln had no idea how long he had been standing in silence, his mind wrapped in the darkness of a cold morning. But when Ambrose Lincoln suddenly crawled out of the black depths of his subconscious and saw the faint reflection of a gray light pressed against the windowpane, he was alone. The room was empty.

He was clutching a 9 mm Luger and could not remember holding one before. Yet, it seemed so comfortable in his grip. Somewhere far away, he thought he heard the whistle of a distant train, and the smell of gunpowder burned sharply in his nostrils.

Lincoln glanced down at the Luger and noticed that the pistol was loaded. He had never had any doubts that it would be.

He glanced around the room.

It was, as George Fitzgerald told him, empty. It did not look as though Robert Priestly had ever spent the night there. Not even the dust on the table had been disturbed.

Ambrose Lincoln knew where the ticket would be hidden unless, of course, Robert Priestly had disappeared without ever stepping into room five twenty-six.

He had been trained to know.

He could hear the words now.

Harsh.

And brittle.

Lincoln walked briskly across the floor and opened the top drawer of the table. He removed a Bible.

It was all in the room number.

Five.

Two.

Six.

He found the fifth book of the Bible, Joshua. He turned to the second chapter and read the sixth verse: *But she had brought them up to the roof of the house and hid them with the stalks of flax, which she had laid in order upon the roof.*

Ambrose Lincoln took the staircase to the rooftop.

There were no stalks of flax.

But there was a stack of scrap lumber beside the brick chimney.

He found the ticket tied with cord to the lumber.

It had a name and the name of a town.

He had seen the name before: *Rachel Gruner.*

The town was *Baden-Baden.*

Ambrose Lincoln walked out of the St. Regis Hotel while darkness still lay heavy upon the District of Columbia. He caught a taxi to the airport. He had a German Heckler & Koch P7 9 mm self-loading automatic pistol in his satchel and a 9 mm Luger in his belt. He would not require any additional luggage.

24.

THE SHADOWS WERE her hiding place. Rachel Gruner had followed them into the alley, and she lay against a crumbling brick wall, waiting for the tumult and the shouting to die away, provided it would ever end, and she feared that the screams and the gunshots would never end.

Angry voices barked orders.

The fearful whimpered.

She didn't know when it happened, but after a while, Rachel realized that all of the voices had been silenced. And she heard the whining, complaining engines of the trucks fade away in the night.

She waited, afraid to move, almost afraid to breathe.

She waited for the German officer to find her.

He stood at the entrance of the alleyway, then casually leaned against the wall and calmly lit a cigarette. Rachel could not see his face, only his eyes, and they burned as red as coals in the dim glow of the streetlight.

His arm hung loosely at his side, clutching a pistol.

He suddenly raised it to shoulder level and fired.

The bullet blasted through a garbage can and ricocheted along the bricks and into the gutter.

Now was the German officer's turn to wait.

He stared intently into the alley.

Nothing moved.

He took one step into the darkness, hesitated for a moment, then backed away. Apparently satisfied that the girl had eluded him or was dead, the officer turned abruptly and strode back out into the dying turmoil that had been running rampant throughout the ruins of the little Jewish marketplace. He paused just long enough to reach down, pick up a silver pendant from the street, and thrust it into his pocket.

Rachel watched him climb arrogantly into his jeep, reload his pistol, then ride away, cutting back across the tattered remnants that had been left in disarray across a neighborhood that had died and burned.

What had taken years to build was gone in hours.

Sometimes in minutes.

Rachel's knee hurt where she had fallen.

It was swollen slightly, and the bruise was beginning to turn purple. She limped back out into the street and looked immediately for a glimpse of the brown shirts.

They were gone.

The trucks had left.

The dead had been carried to the steps of the synagogue that was only the gaunt skeletal remains of brick and lumber.

No one came to claim them. Those who knew them, and those who loved them lay among them.

Or they, too, were gone.

Only a few had ventured out into the ruins, walking on broken glass with bare and bleeding feet. All Rachel saw were the haunted, beaten faces of strangers who had nothing left, who had been cast adrift in a world that made no sense. It wasn't the world they had made, simply the one they had inherited.

For them, she knew, there would be no escape.

She could see it in their eyes.

They had clung to hope when the glass starting breaking in the streets around them. They had clung to their faith when the flames began pouring out of the synagogue. They had clung to their courage when the gunshot disrupted the night.

Now it was all gone.

Hope.

Faith.

Courage.

Rachel found the aging Samuel Feichtmann sitting on the curb in front of his bakeshop, his head in his hands. He glanced up at her as she sat down beside him.

"Your father?" he asked.

Rachel shook her head.

Feichtmann did not appear surprised. He sighed deeply. His eyes were red. He would have cried, but he had cried all night, and no one had come to dry the tears. "It's just as well," he said. "Your father was a good and kind man, and now he has escaped all of this."

"Where is everyone?" Rachel asked. "I see faces, but I don't recognize any of the faces. They are not our faces."

"They are coming to replace us."

"Why?" Rachel asked.

Feichtmann shrugged. "Someone came to replace them," he said.

"What has happened to us?" she asked.

"The old are dead or dying," he said. "The young men have all been carried away."

"Where are the Germans taking them?"

"Poland is the word I hear when people are talking on the streets."

"Why Poland?"

"In Poland, the Germans have places to work them." He sighed again. "In Poland," Feichtmann continued, "the Germans have places to kill them."

"Why do the Germans want us dead?"

"Why does the boot step on the cockroach?" Feichtmann slumped his shoulders. It was a resignation of surrender. His was a question that did not need an answer.

The faint light of morning was beginning to crease the sky. The rain had moved elsewhere, but still there was no hint of sunshine. A cold numbness had set in. Rachel shivered. "Why did no one come to help us?" she asked.

"No one ever comes to help the Jews."

"We are still people," Rachel said adamantly.

"To the Germans," Feichtmann answered, "we should have never left the Old Testament."

She reached over and placed a gentle hand on Feichtmann's shoulder. "Don't worry," she said. "As long as we have breath, we have life. We will rise up and begin anew." Rachel smiled. "We always do."

"Not this time."

"Why not?"

Feichtmann stood and began walking slowly up the street. "This time, there are not enough of us left to begin again."

Rachel called after him. "Where are you going?"

"To bury the dead," he said. "And wait until I join them. I don't think it will be a long wait."

She ran to his side and grabbed his arm. He stopped in a street littered with broken glass and spent cartridge shells. "The Germans have gone," she said.

Feichtmann turned away and refused to look at her. He sadly shook his head. "The Germans are never gone," he said.

25.

HE WAS A big man, broad but not tall, with a polished bald head that glistened from the fractured reflection of light falling from a large, faceted crystal ball hanging above the Shoreham Hotel ballroom in downtown Washington. He sat in a dark corner on the west side of the room, out of the way and strangely inconspicuous among the cast of outsiders who had paid ridiculous amounts of money to hear President Franklin Roosevelt lead them out of an economic depression that had strangled their country. They would go home with their signature programs and little else, but that was good enough.

The big man preferred to be far removed the political prostitutes, the power brokers, the movers and shakers who clustered as close to the dais as they could get. The air in the hotel was thick with cigar smoke, and it rose toward the brass chandelier, turning a pale blue before it touched the ceiling.

A band was playing loudly.

The big man did not notice.

The waiter wearing a rented tux kept a face of stone as he sat a glass of Benedictine mixed with Brandy on the table before him. The big man had his eyes set on a small cadre of second-rate, hometown politicians scurrying around the podium, making sure that everything was in its proper place before FDR himself walked out into the spotlight. No mistakes would be tolerated. He glanced at his watch and squinted in the dim light. He had six minutes to wait if the show started on time, and it hardly ever did.

Atticus Chandler wore a perpetual scowl. His face was square and had a ruddy complexion as though he had spent the afternoon on the bow of a sailboat in the Chesapeake. He had. He wore a deep gray suit with thin pinstripes whether he was in the office or not. He made it a point to never stand out in a crowd. He fit quite nicely and unobtrusively in the social circles of political aristocracy. He did not appear to be among the very rich. Then again, he had never been mistaken for a member of the working class either.

He knew which hands to shake.

He knew which cheeks to kiss.

He knew the names of the big money boys.

It was his job to know where they kept their skeletons and the deadliest of their dark secrets. Some he had personally removed and hidden for them. Atticus Chandler never dug any graves, but he chose the cemeteries.

He knew whose debts had been paid, whose bank accounts were hanging in limbo, and who were still in debt, and to whom. In the business of politics, money had never been as important as raw ambition, which could be bought but was more often taken by force and an unquenchable thirst for power. Men lived for it and died for it. Atticus Chandler remained cloaked in the shadows. He was the man they feared, the man who didn't exist. He watched the games they played in the sanctity of the Capitol anterooms. Atticus Chandler kept score.

He saw Rudolph Hinkel come into the ballroom, stood without attracting any attention, and began walking toward him, careful to remain in the shadows hugging the wall. Neither man spoke. With a nod, Atticus motioned the German industrialist into the dark sanctity of the bar.

Not even a President like Roosevelt could disturb their conversation as they seated themselves at a back table. A single candle was burning on the table. Atticus reached over and snuffed it out with his fingers. Black, he thought, was a good color on him.

Rudolph Hinkel was, at first glance, a man of great wealth. His suit had been custom made by the best tailor in Washington. Atticus knew. He had paid for the suit. The businessman had a square face, carved from flawed granite, and a thick head of gray hair. He had come to hear Roosevelt only because Atticus Chandler had sent him an invitation. It was obviously a wasted invitation.

There were no pleasantries, no small talk. Atticus got right to the point. "Tell me about this Adolph fellow you have running your country," he said.

"He has power," Hinkel said. "He has charm. He can hypnotize a thousand men or a single woman. He is a leader. Whatever he says, his countrymen will follow him to a grave or to the edge of the world. You have never seen the likes of Adolph Hitler before."

"I hear he's a crazy sonuvabitch," Atticus said.

"He does have his idiosyncrasies."

Atticus leaned over the table and asked in a low, sandpaper voice, "What does he want?"

"I'm not sure I understand."

"It sounds to me like the bastard wants a war."

"He only wants to build Germany," Hinkel said.

"I hear he wants to rule the goddam world."

"If it's good for Germany, he will." Hinkel's face was solemn.

"You tell Hitler I don't want a goddam war," Atticus said.

"He does not listen to me."

"He damn well better," Atticus said. He leaned back in his chair and reached for his glass of Benedictine and Brandy. "This country does a helluva lot of business with your country. Your country has gotten rich off my country. A goddam war will leave us both broke."

"Hitler can build Germany quite well and quite large without either your money or your markets," Hinkel said. He voice was hollow. "You must remember, Mister Chandler, the United States needs Germany a lot more than Germany needs the United States."

He didn't believe it. They were words off a written script. Atticus was sure of it. He emptied his glass and spoke slowly and through clenched teeth. "You can tell Adolph he won't be able to piss on either side of the Rhine if he starts a war that we don't want."

Hinkel opened his mouth to answer.

He had nothing to say.

"Tell me," Atticus said, "what the hell's going on in Baden-Baden?"

"What have your heard?"

"I hear Hitler's trying to kick the Jews out of Austria."

"That's a problem we both have," Hinkel replied.

"What's that?"

"Your newspapers lie to you, and our newspapers lie to us."

"Our newspapers have said damn little about it."

Hinkel allowed himself to smile. "There's very little to say about it," he said. He shrugged. "A Jewish lad shot and killed a German officer working in the German Embassy," he said. "A few of the young German boys went to protest. They threw a few rocks and broke a few windows. Nothing more."

"Where was the embassy?"

"Which embassy?"

"The one where the German officer was killed."

"Paris."

"Where was this protest?"

Hinkel paused. He sighed. "Baden-Baden," he said softly.

"You have bad numbers, Rudolph, and they don't add up."

"I told you what I know."

Atticus nodded. "Now let me tell you what I know," he said. "You and me, whether this Adolph Hitler likes it or not, must not go to war. You make damn sure he doesn't do a damn thing to draw us into a conflict that could break both of us. We got a lot of ocean between us, Rudolph. Let's keep it that way."

He stood and eased out the back door before the applause had ended for the introduction of President Franklin D. Roosevelt.

26.

AMBROSE LINCOLN HAD taken the first train leaving the District of Columbia. He knew he should have felt some remorse for George Fitzgerald or least regret for his sudden demise. But reality was reality, even in the shadows of a fragmented mind. Fitzgerald had left the organization and walked into a bullet. Maybe, for him, it was better that way. Maybe it was better for him to die once and quickly than face the fear of dying every day of his life.

Poor George.

He had been a pawn in a deadly game.

Nothing more.

Nothing less.

George Fitzgerald had not been a fixer.

He only came to town and made arrangements. Arrive early. Leave early. Don't look back. Don't ask questions.

If someone dies, sign the death certificate.

Make sure he's buried.

Then go.

He knew nothing.

Then again, maybe still he knew too much.

The man was taking no chances.

He gave the orders. Ambrose could almost hear his voice.

Harsh.

And brittle.

When Gretchen Sloane buried George Fitzgerald, she buried his secrets with him, if he had any at all. George Fitzgerald had not expected to die. He would never know why he died. Some questions are better left unanswered.

Ambrose Lincoln had walked out of the St. Regis with a note he had found on the roof of the hotel and a folder that Robert Priestly had mailed to himself, that Dr. Sloane had taken from Fitzgerald, that Lincoln found folded in his coat pocket.

The note had a single name: *Rachel Gruner.*

The note listed a single town: *Baden-Baden.*

The folder held a single telegram: It's not what you think. Stop. It's not what you think you know. Stop. They are hiding the truth. Stop. They have buried the truth. Stop. The pictures don't lie. Stop. America must know. Stop. The truth must not die with them.

Ambrose Lincoln had no idea what the message meant.

But he would learn what it meant and why it had been sent.

Ambrose Lincoln was a fixer.

And deep within his subconscious, he heard again the voice of the man, yet Lincoln could not remember when they met or why they met. His words didn't make sense then.   They still didn't.

"You are a fixer," the voice said.

Lincoln had not spoken.

But his eyes had asked the question.

The voice answered.

"You will find what is broken."

Lincoln had nodded.

"Then you will fix it."

"How will I know what's broken?" Lincoln had asked.

"We'll find it for you."

"And if I can't fix it?"

The voice had not answered him.

But when Lincoln opened his eyes, the voice and the man were gone. Ambrose Lincoln was alone.

Maybe the voice and the man hadn't been in the room at all.

He sat in the darkness. And waited.

He waited for the nurse to come and take him again to a room where electrodes would be strapped to his brain again.

But the doctor was German.
The prison was outside Berlin.
He had been a soldier.
How had he been captured?
Where had he been captured?
Why did he remember the voice so clearly?
And why was the voice speaking English?
And why was he on a train to Baltimore?
And how did he know what to do next?
And why did he know anything at all?

On the back of the telegram, Robert Priestly – it must have been Priestly – had scratched a phone number.

Lincoln had called it.

"Baltimore," a soft voice said.

It may have been a woman.

"Diffendahl Airport."

"The time."

"The plane will be there when you arrive."

"Does it have a schedule."

"You are the schedule," the voice said.

The phone went dead.

It was still at least three hours before daylight by the time Ambrose Lincoln departed the train, ran down a taxi, and traveled to the airfield just outside of Essex and across the bay from Baltimore. He had not slept on the train.

He could not remember the last time he slept.

He stepped out of the taxi, left five dollars on the seat, and walked toward a Pan American Boeing 314 that waited in the darkness at the far end of the runway.

The captain climbed down the steps to meet him.

"Are you my cargo?" he asked

"I am."

"You must be somebody damn important," the captain said.

"Not particularly."

"I have orders to get you to Europe."

"It's better than Peoria," Lincoln said.

"And these are the things you must remember," the captain said. "This plane doesn't exist, this flight doesn't exist, and I don't exist." The captain shrugged. "And the second you leave this plane and set foot on Polish soil, you don't exist either. This whole night is just a figment of our imagination."

"How long is the flight?" Lincoln asked.

"As near as I can figure, it's somewhere on either side of twenty-nine hours."

"You don't know for sure?"

The captain shook his head.

"Why not?"

"We've never wrestled this hunk of metal across the Atlantic before."

"If we go down," Lincoln said, "I have one favor to ask."

"What 's that?"

"Don't wake me up."

Lincoln walked on the plane and glanced down the aisle. On the back seat, staring at him with cold, unwavering eyes was a man of obvious wealth and means. A square face that looked as though it had been carved from flawed granite. Gray hair. Tailored suit. Unlike Lincoln, he didn't need a shave.

"I guess I'm not the only cargo you're hauling tonight," Lincoln said.

"I'm not for sure where your orders came from," the captain said. "But his came from the White House."

"We both going to the same place?"

"If we get that far, I'm only landing this sonovabitch once," the captain said as he shut the door and shut out the faint sounds of a Maryland night.

27.

AMBROSE LINCOLN HAD no idea how long he slept, but when he awoke, he had the odd sensation of a world slowly falling apart around him. A storm had risen up above the Atlantic, and the winds were tossing the big Boeing 314 around the sky as though it were a paper kite in a hurricane.

The string of running lights flickered in the cabin, and the darkness outside the plane was a constant staccato of lightning bolts dancing from cloud to cloud. Lincoln wondered if it would be their last dance. They were dangling like metal puppets in the sky, and someone had reached down and cut their strings.

They would go down, and no one would find them.

They would go down, and no one would look for them.

The captain had already explained it as succinctly as he could.

The flight doesn't exist, he had said back on the runway. *The plane doesn't exist. None of us exist.*

Ambrose Lincoln forced an ironic smile.

He hadn't existed for a long time.

Even now, his papers and his passport said he was Klaus Wagner.

But then, his life, for as long as he could remember, and he often had trouble remembering past day before yesterday, had been one lie after another.

He might as well believe the lies.

There was nothing else for him to believe in.

He glanced at the newspaper on the seat beside him. It had been folded to page sixteen, section A.

There at the bottom, with a small two-column headline, was the story about some ruffians roaming through small towns in Germany and Austria. They were protesting the murder of a German diplomat by a Jewish firebrand.

That's what the story said. Some vandalism. Some broken glass. A few fires. Nothing serious. Nothing that mattered.

For a moment, Lincoln closed his eyes and remembered the young woman who met him on the train.

They will tell you lies, she said. *The politicians will tell you lies. The newspapers will tell you lies.*

Now he saw the lies in newsprint.

Now, he understood.

Lincoln leaned out into the aisle and looked toward the back of the plane. The man with a square face and gray hair was still staring at him.

No smile.

No blink.

No flicker of recognition.

But the stare had not left him since the plane left Essex. Lincoln was sure of it.

He nodded toward the man. "Rough night," he said.

The square faced man who had arrived on orders from the White House did not answer him.

His arms were folded in defiance.

He wore a perpetual scowl.

Ambrose Lincoln ignored him.

But he would not forget him.

He looked through the cockpit door. A sudden flash of lightning illuminated the pilot's face.

His chin was resting on his chest.

His head was cocked to one side.

And he was whistling some tune that might have come from Glenn Miller if Miller had been drunk and playing a tuba instead of a trombone.

The storm was not bothering him at all.

Lincoln removed his seat belt, stood, and worked his way up the aisle as the wind pitched him and the plane rudely from one side to the other.

He knelt behind the Captain. "Not a very good night," he said.

"Do me a favor," the Captain said.

"Sure, what is it?"

"Look out the window."

Lincoln did.

"Is the sky above us?" the Captain asked.

"It is."

"Is the ground beneath us?"

"Seems to be."

The Captain shrugged. "It's a good night," he said.

"This is not your first time to make this run, is it?" Lincoln said.

"What run are you talking about?"

"New York to wherever in Europe we're going."

"You've got it all wrong," the Captain said. "When we go to Europe, it's by ship. Takes several days and sometime several weeks. We don't fly to Europe. Ask anybody. We don't have a plane that'll make it that far."

"I guess this is just a figment of my imagination."

"If you have an imagination, it is."

"And if I don't."

"Won't make any difference."

"Why not?"

"The boys who get off my plane don't come back."

A wind gust pitched the plane roughly aside as the pilot fought to bring it under control. His jaws were rigid, his teeth clenched, every muscle in his arms were straining to keep the plane as far as possible above the water.

Lincoln had been thrown face down in the floor.

The Luger spilled from his pocket.

The pilot caught a glimpse of it. "You better go back and strap yourself in," he said. "I have a feeling it's gonna get rough before we get there."

"You flying this thing by yourself?"

"You see a co-pilot."

"No."

"I guess I'm by myself."

Lincoln nodded. "Most of us are," he said.

He pulled himself to his feet and fought his way back up the aisle. He suddenly stopped.

He knew the cargo consisted of two passengers.

He hadn't expected a third.

He saw the woman sitting on the far side of the plane, her head bowed as if in prayer. He squinted to make out her facial features in the dim, flickering lights.

She was no stranger.

He was sure of it.

He had seen her before.

Lincoln's eyes fell on the small, oval face of a young woman, maybe thirty, maybe not, with long raven hair and a beauty mark or a spot of mud under her left eye. She was barely five feet tall and wore a woolen dress the color of the earth. Her skin was pale, translucent, and had not yet been touched by the sun. She was barefoot and carrying a bleached cotton sack. Her eyes were dark, filled with bitterness and regret.

She looked toward him and smiled.

It was a sad smile.

They were lying, she had told him on the train.

They were hiding the truth. That's what the telegram had said.

But who were they?

And what was the lie?

And who knew the truth?

And must he kill to find it?

Or must he die to keep it hidden.

Ambrose Lincoln slumped in his seat.

The lights went out, and the plane was swallowed in darkness.

A single flash of lightning poured into the window where the woman was sitting.

It flashed again.

She was gone.

28.

ATTICUS CHANDLER HAD been greatly troubled by the telegram he had received from Berlin. It had arrived at his downtown Washington apartment at two-thirty in the morning and was marked *Urgent.* He read it once, then again. Atticus Chandler had not slept the rest of the night.

The telegram's message was as oblique as he would have expected it to be. But Atticus was an old pro at reading between the lines.

He had read:

Worse than reported. Stop. Rumors are truth. Stop. Camera found. Stop. Film missing. Stop.

It had not been signed.

It didn't matter.

Atticus Chandler knew who sent it.

He never drank at three in the morning, but he poured himself Benedictine and Brandy. The liquid splashed over the rim of the glass. He doubted if it would calm his nerves. Then again, it couldn't hurt.

Atticus sat back in the darkness of his study and closed his eyes. A dull ache was slowly working its way behind his temples.

His head throbbed.

A sharp pain cut into his chest.

Indigestion, he thought.

It couldn't be his heart.

Atticus laughed.

He didn't have a heart. That's what his enemies said anyway.

All he had in the early morning hours were questions.

Who was the photographer?

Had he taken photographs during the Night of Broken Glass?

What was on those photographs?

Would the pictures be an indictment against the Germans?

He shuddered.

Did those images hold the truth?

Or did they simply show only the face of some old man's granddaughter?

He gripped the telegram tightly and felt a hot rage rising up within him. Atticus knew he could not afford to take any chances. War must be prevented at all costs. His business depended on it. His fortune depended on it.

He said down and wrote a succinct reply:

Film must be found. Stop. Film must be destroyed. Stop. Remove all eyes who have seen the film or knows it exists. Stop.

Atticus Chandler lumbered across the hallway to his bedroom, threw his robe aside and began dressing in the same suit he had worn to meet Rudolph Henkel under the guise of hearing the President's speech. This time, however, he didn't bother with the tie. He tied his shoe laces and reached for his wool overcoat.

He could trust no one.

Not now.

He would deliver the message to the telegraph office himself.

It was still snowing as he drove out into the street.

He cursed the weather.

He cursed his bad fortune.

He cursed the Germans.

If anyone could find the missing film, Leopold could.

Leopold had long been his eyes in Europe. And there was something about Leopold that had always intrigued him.

Leopold didn't have a conscience.

Atticus Chandler knew it was absolutely vital to keep the truth about Hitler's orchestrated sweep through Baden-Baden a secret.

It was a truth that America did not want to face or deal with.

Atticus had to confront it, no matter how ugly the truth might be or had become.

He had no choice.

The truth was a terrible burden to bear.

Leopold had sent his first message while the smoke was still pouring thick through the Jewish section of the town.

Germans attacked, it said.

Businesses ruined, it said.

Homes burned, it said.

Streets covered with broken glass, it said.

Men sent away to prison, it said.

Women killed, it said.

Children dying, it said.

The warm blood coursing through Atticus Chandler's veins had run cold. America would not concern itself with a few businesses being vandalized, a few homes on fire, streets littered with shards of glass. That was Europe's problem, and Americans lumped all of the countries into a single word: Europe.

The people occupying those far away unknown and unfamiliar countries had never gotten along.

Governments had to crack down from time to time. If governments used force to fight back against violence, it was their business and probably necessary.

The newspapers in Washington and New York had only printed a few random paragraphs in a few random stories about the night of broken glass, a catchy phrase that signified nothing, not in America anyway. But Americans must not know about the women and children dying.

Especially the children.

Americans must not see the photographs of the horror that tormented the Jews that night.

Words could be denied.

Rumors would fade away.

But the photograph of a dead child lying in the streets of Baden-Baden with a German brown shirt marching in the background would condemn them all.

Americans would rise up in arms.

Roosevelt, Atticus knew, had never been regarded as a hawk. He was obviously aware of the unrest. But war was the farthest thing from his mind.

Yet, the President must never be allowed to see the photographs. Any response from Roosevelt would be a travesty. It could cost Atticus Chandler millions. It wouldn't do his business with Germany any good either.

Atticus, quite simply, would not allow it to happen. Leopold would make sure of it. The film would burn as easily as the synagogue.

29.

AMBROSE LINCOLN WATCHED the snow-blanketed patch of earth rise up to meet the plane as daylight fought its way past a bank of thunderheads. His muscles were tight, and his joints ached. Seventeen hours in an angry sky can do that to a man. This marked the second time the Boeing 314 had gone down. The first landing had been for fuel only. He assumed the Tin Goose was running low on fuel again. He assumed the stop had been charted and planned.

Then somewhere in the back recesses of his mind, he heard the voice again.

Harsh.

And brittle.

Men who assume things are men who make mistakes, and men who make mistakes are men who lie in forgotten graves.

"Where are we?" Lincoln asked as the plane rolled to a stop

"On the ground," the captain said as roughly as he felt.

"This place have a name?"

"It's best if you don't know.

Lincoln arched an eyebrow. It was an unasked question.

"If you don't know, " the captain said, "then you can't tell anyone what you don't know even if they kill you, and they will."

"Who?"

The captain shrugged.

"You'll know soon enough," he said as he climbed down from the cockpit and shuffled across the tarmac toward a small building that set back on the ragged edge of darkness. No lights had illuminated the runway. The pilot had come down flying blind. But then, it obviously wasn't his first flight across the Atlantic.

Ambrose Lincoln unstrapped himself and walked up the aisle. He leaned out the door and yelled, "How long are we here?"

"Till I finish."

"What?"

"The soup."

"What kind?"

"It's never made me sick," the pilot said and bowed his head into a stiff wind blowing out of the north.

Lincoln followed him across the tarmac. A bitter chill hung in the air, and there were faint traces of sleet stinging his face.

He had looked back over his shoulder before leaving the plane. The man with the square face and gray hair had not moved in his seat.

He was sleeping.

Or dead.

Lincoln didn't know.

Nor did he care.

The café was small, a single counter with four stools. Lincoln sat down beside the pilot and nodded at the waitress, pushing forty-five and still pretty with auburn hair braided across the top of her head. She smiled.

It was a reflex.

"Order the soup," the pilot said.

"Why?"

"It comes with a knife."

He shrugged. "A man can always use a knife."

"Is this a military base?" Lincoln asked.

The captain turned and looked at him with a strange grin on his face. "You're not a very fast learner," he said.

"What makes you say that?"

"This place doesn't exist," the captain said.

"And I'm not here."

The captain nodded toward the waitress. "See Lucille," he said.

Lincoln nodded.

"She won't remember you." He laughed. "Hell, she won't even remember me, and I married her."

"When?"

"She doesn't remember, and I no longer give a damn."

The soup was hot and thick. Chunks of potatoes. Strips of tomatoes. A batch of barley. And nodules of meat, mostly fat. The gravy stock was a strange shade of green.

"It doesn't look good," the captain said. "It doesn't particularly smell good. I try to swallow as much of it as I can without tasting it. But when you're hungry and haven't eaten in a week, and somebody keeps ramming a night stick down your throat, you'd kill for a bowl."

"Not me," Lincoln said.

"Just wait."

"I'd kill for nothing."

The captain sat back on his stool and carefully measured Ambrose Lincoln with weary eyes.

"Is that what you do?" he asked.

"What?"

"Kill for nothing."

"They say I did."

"Who's they?"

"They didn't say."

The captain swallowed another spoonful of hot soup and wiped his mouth with the back of his hand.

"Is that why I'm taking you to Poland."

"No."

"I know it's not a pleasure trip." The pilot laughed again. "I don't fly pleasure junkets."

"I'm looking for someone."

"You have a reason?"

"Not until I find them."

The captain wiped his hands on a towel and pushed back off the stool. "We might as well get that junkyard of metal up and running again," he said.

"We still have a good piece to go before I get to sleep again."

Ambrose Lincoln drained his bowl.

He had not tasted a bite.

He never did.

"Don't forget to look under the bowl," the pilot said.

"What's there?"

"The knife."

The knife had been taped in place, small enough to hide in the wrinkles of his jacket, sharp as a razor blade.

"It'll come in handy when they take your Luger away."

"I don't plan on losing the Luger," Lincoln said.

"That's what they all say," the captain said as he walked briskly back out into the wind. The sleet was coming down harder now. "And that's how we bury them."

"How?"

"Without the Luger." He shrugged. "Men who die unarmed are men who die naked," he said.

Lincoln stopped. He had heard the words before.

They had been harsh.

And brittle.

The captain was climbing into the plane, and Lincoln was standing alone on the runway. It was a cold day to die, he thought. He shrugged. It was also a cold day to live.

30.

THE SNOW WAS blinding as night began to fade to daylight. Ambrose Lincoln did not catch a glimpse of the blurred runway until the wheels of the Clipper were getting ready to touch the gravel tarmac. He had no idea how the pilot had been able to find such a narrow landing strip. The captain was slumped in his seat, chewing on a toothpick and battling the wind, the snow, and a short runway that came to a dead end at the base of a cliff. Ambrose Lincoln did not see the mountains until he had climbed down from the Boeing 314, and even then they were little more than scattered bits and pieces of green outlined against a gray November sky.

The square faced man with gray hair pulled his woolen coat tightly around his throat and hurried down from the plane, walking briskly to the far side of the tarmac where a black limousine sat waiting for him.

"You think they'll give me a ride?" Lincoln asked the pilot.

"You know the President?"

"No."

"You vote for him?"

"Don't remember."

"Then they don't see you," the Captain said. "This plane delivered one package of cargo this morning. He's it. Straight from the White House. You don't exist. You were added to the manifesto at the last minute."

He shrugged. "You weren't on board. You won't be walking away when I leave. Those in the car didn't see you. As far as the cargo was concerned, you came along to clean the plane. You don't look for him, and he won't look for you. It's better that way."

"Are there other cars?" Lincoln asked as he and the pilot stood in the blizzard, letting the snow bank up against their legs.

"Looks like you're on your own," the Captain said.

"Where do I find transportation?"

"Katowice." The pilot nodded toward the mountains. "You'll find the main road about six hundred yards through the cut," he said. "The city is about five miles north down the road, or about two miles if you go through the mountain pass."

"You think I'll be able to find the pass in this weather?"

The pilot shook his head. "Not a chance," he said.

Lincoln watched the red taillight of the limousine fade white, then disappear.

"I guess I'll take the road," he said.

"If a car stops for you, don't get in," the pilot said.

"Why not?"

"They'll shoot you."

"They won't get much."

"They aren't looking for much."

Ambrose Lincoln began walking across the runway. A harsh wind rolled out of the highlands in violent bursts. The cold only hurt for a moment. By the time he reached the cut that led toward the main road, he was numb.

He paused, turned around, and nodded to the Captain.

"I have one word of advice," the pilot yelled before the winds could tear his words away.

"What's that?"

"When you get to the train station in Katowice, let them take the Luger."

"They won't find it."

"They must find it."

"Why?"

"If they find the Luger, they'll be satisfied." The captain grinned. "If they find the Luger, they won't look for the automatic pistol you have in your boot. And if they shoot you, neither weapon will do you any good. Let them take the Luger."

"How did you know about the pistol?"

The Captain shrugged. "I don't know you. I don't want to know you. I don't know why you're here. I don't want to know why you're here." He paused, then added, "But I have a pretty good idea who sent you."

Lincoln nodded.

"Then you know more than I do," he said.

Mostly, he said it to himself.

By the time Lincoln reached the road, he could hear the roar of the engines in the background. The plane was rolling down the runway, headed into the wind. A low, angry grumble carved its way up the side of the mountains, holding steady until the world around him was swaddled in silence.

The snow made no sound when it touched the ground.

Even the winds had died to a whisper.

He was alone again.

Lincoln headed north. Only his feet were able to tell him that he was still on the roadway. He could no longer see the pavement. It had been buried by snow. From the looks of it, the road had been buried for days.

Lincoln calculated that it would take him three hours, maybe a little less, to reach Katowice.

It took four.

The streets were jammed with trucks, mostly military, and the back ends were jammed with human fodder. Young men with tired and hollow eyes stared back at him. He had seen the look before, usually on faces packed into coffins and placed by the side of the road, waiting for the graveyard crew to find them and haul them away. Some lay there a week. The look never changed.

Lincoln pushed his way through the crowd on the sidewalk. Old women with their baskets of bread. Old men with their pipes. Soldiers with eyes as deadly as the rifles they carried. But beneath the façade, they were like everyone else adrift in the town square.

They were scared.

Ambrose Lincoln was wary of the scared.

They would kill before they knew they had pulled the trigger.

They would kill because they expected to die.

Most of them were right.

He eased closer to the walls of the brick buildings, out of the snow, out of the way. No one stopped him. No one looked his way. He was no different from the rest: cold, weary, hungry, suspicious, and uncertain, with the two-day growth of whiskers on his face sprinkled with ice and snow. No one worried about Ambrose Lincoln. He was little more than a stranger among strangers, trapped in lockstep with those lost in a purgatory that imprisoned only the wayward and the misplaced.

He heard the whistle of a train before he saw the station.

One train was leaving.

Another had just eased to a stop alongside the loading platform.

Only one man stood between him and the station's ticket office, a tall German soldier in a heavy gray woolen coat and armed with a standard issue Karabiner 98k. He wiped the snow from his eyes and had a scowl on his face.

He stepped toward Lincoln. "Name," he said.

"Klaus Wagner."

"Papers."

Lincoln handed him his passport.

The soldier's eyes never left Lincoln's face.

"Destination."

"Baden-Baden."

"There are no trains to Baden-Baden."

"I change in Strasbourg."

"Reason for travel to Baden-Baden."

"Business."

"What is your business?"

"I am a teacher."

The soldier reached out, swept Lincoln's jacket open, and ripped the Luger from his belt.

He stared at the pistol. A slow grin etched its way across his face.

He jammed the barrel of the Luger hard against Lincoln's forehead.

"I think you are lying," he said.

31.

AMBROSE LINCOLN DIDN'T blink. He felt the cold steel of the Luger's barrel pressed into the wrinkles of his forehead and knew it could all be over in those split seconds it took for the German sentry to pull the trigger and the pistol to fire.

The thought of death did not particularly concern Lincoln.

He often thought he had been dead for years.

They killed him when they strapped the electrodes to his brain.

They just didn't stop his heart from beating.

But Lincoln thought of the name he had found on the roof of the St. Regis Hotel, the name Robert Priestly had left for him.

Rachel Gruner.

Who was she?

Why was he looking for her?

What did she know?

What could she tell him?

Was she in hiding?

And where would he find her?

She was expecting him.

Whether she knew it or not, she was hoping that someone would be coming for her.

Ambrose Lincoln was as good as the next man.

At times, he was better.

He did not mind dying.

But he did not want to disappoint Rachel Gruner.

Ambrose Lincoln narrowed his eyes, and he heard the sentry speaking again.

"You are no teacher," he said. "I think you are lying. It is a grave mistake to tell lies to the Reich."

The German's eyes were bright and beginning to dilate. A sudden rush of unbridled adrenaline had shot through his veins. His hands were trembling. He had killed from afar. He had hidden in trenches and behind hedgerows and shot down soldiers who had no names and no faces, only forms marching across an empty field.

Now he must kill face to face.

Now he must kill close enough to smell the garlic on the dying man's breath.

Now he must kill close enough to watch life depart from a man's eyes. He hesitated.

A man who hesitates always dies long before his appointed time.

Ambrose Lincoln had heard the words so many times before.

Harsh.

And brittle.

In one swift and fluid motion, Lincoln slipped the thin knife with the blade of a razor from the wrinkles of his jacket collar and sliced the soldier's throat.

As silent as the snowfall.

The sentry coughed once.

His eyes turned to milk.

Lincoln pulled him quickly into an alley and left the German guard lying in a heap of quivering flesh between piles of wooden boxes and decaying trash, the snow turning red beneath him. By the time he walked out of the darkness of the alley, the blood had frozen to the ground.

Lincoln shoved the Luger into his belt, this time in the small of his back, replaced the knife in the folds of his jacket, and stepped out into the snow.

Those who passed by him had not seen a thing.

If they did see, they did not care.

If they had seen, they only walked a little faster.

The sentry's death was not on their conscience.

Neither would it affect the way Ambrose Lincoln slept that night. He did not choose the men he killed.

Lincoln sighed deeply.

They volunteered.

They always did.

He had learned the harsh moments of reality that separated life from death so long ago.

He had learned it with electrodes piercing his brain.

Lincoln crossed the street, pushed his way into the depot, presented his passport, and purchased a ticket for Klaus Wagner to Baden-Baden with a two-hour change of trains in Strasbourg.

He paid cash.

The ticket was one way.

His plans did not include the future. He did not plan his movements from one day to tomorrow.

Ambrose Lincoln lived in a single moment. And it always surprised him when one moment spilled into the next. Each breath was unexpected. Another breath was a gift.

He certainly had not bought it.

The train to Strasbourg rolled out of Katowice at sixteen minutes after three o'clock. He sat in the chill of a gray afternoon. Outside, the snow continued to assault the Austrian countryside. The wind whistled through a crack in the window. It was much like the moan of a woman in pain.

A German officer sat across from him.

An Austrian businessman walked into the small, cramped compartment, took one look at the Nazi uniform, and sat down beside Ambrose Lincoln. His face had been burned by the cold and the wind. He had a woolen hat with the brim pulled low over his face.

His eyes had been running.

His bulbous nose was swollen.

He looked at Lincoln and forced a smile.

Lincoln turned away.

The businessman introduced himself.

Lincoln did not respond. He folded his arms and closed his eyes.

He had shut out the day.

He had shut out the cold.

He had shut out the last whimpers a man made before his death.

Now he was shutting out the businessman.

The businessman leaned toward him and gently cleared his throat. His voice was soft and had a slight quiver.

"I know Rachel," he said.

32.

ATTICUS CHANDLER HAD been awakened by a phone call from the President while most of Washington was still sleeping. Atticus glanced at the clock as he pulled his big frame out of bed. It was thirty-two minutes past four o'clock.

The call was later than usual.

He would not hear the President's voice on the other end.

He never did.

It was not wise for anyone to know that Franklin Roosevelt had ever crossed paths with the likes of Atticus Chandler.

The voice belonged to Samuel Fuller. He was the second most powerful man in Washington, and some said that Fuller served most days as the President's boss. The nation may have elected Roosevelt.

Fuller ran the country.

He controlled the money.

He doled out the power.

This time, he had given it to Roosevelt. Only he had the ability take it away, provided he had a reason. Samuel Fuller could make men or break them with a single phone call.

There was never any blood on his hands. His reputation remained unstained. Atticus Chandler, however, had been washing his hands in blood for a long time.

He may or may not have liked it. That point would be debated for years. But he didn't mind it.

He was paid a salary to do a job.

He did it.

He did it well.

And somewhere along the way, Atticus Chandler had become enormously wealthy. It was surprising, he often thought, how expensive a man's life could be, especially if he were powerful, in Washington, and immersed in politics. The same life in a farm field outside of Wichita would cost no more than a handshake. In the shadow of the capitol, the life was attached to a dollar sign with a multitude of zeros.

Not everyone wanted Atticus Chandler's job.

Not everyone knew Atticus Chandler had a job.

Atticus Chandler held the phone to his ear and listened to the voice on the other end while writing a handful of words down on a notepad that had been placed on a table beside the bed.

The Willard Hotel.

Seven forty-five.

Room two-forty-eight.

Freight elevator.

Atticus met with Samuel Fuller at least twice a month, sometimes more. It was always at the same hotel, the same room, at the same time. It was only a block away from the White House. Close. Convenient. Discreet. Both men knew that it would not be wise for Atticus Chandler to be seen anywhere near the White House.

He was never early.

Or late.

Atticus Chandler knocked on the door exactly at seven forty-five. A colonel, probably retired, pressed and starched in his full dress uniform, opened the door and nodded his recognition. No words were exchanged. He walked out as Atticus walked in.

"Tell me about Europe," Fuller said before Atticus could remove his woolen overcoat and sit down.

"It is simmering," Atticus said.

He dropped down in an overstuffed wingback chair, probably imported from France, probably from the nineteenth century, probably a gift from the Fuller Foundation.

Fuller was lean and wiry with close-cropped gray hair, dressed as though he was going to or coming from a Washington party. His black tie had been loosened, and his ebony cufflinks matched the suit. His face was thin, almost gaunt, and had been erased of all emotion. A pencil thin mustache arched across his lip. It was white and trimmed as neatly as his hair.

"The President doesn't like what he sees happening in Germany," Fuller said. 'This Hitler fellow makes him nervous."

"Most of Europe is nervous."

"Is he going to war?"

"It's just a matter of time."

"The President does not want to be dragged into another war," Fuller said, reaching for a pack of cigarettes on the bed.

"He won't be."

"Do you have eyes in Germany?"

"I do."

"Can you trust them?"

"Implicitly."

Fuller lit a cigarette and took a long slow draw. He leaned his head back and blew a smoke ring toward the ceiling.

"The President keeps reading about an incident in some place called Baden or Baden-Baden."

"What did he read?"

"Some German students got upset when a German diplomat was killed and stormed through a Jewish settlement," Fuller said. "Windows broken. Homes burned down. It could have blown up into quite a fiasco."

"It didn't."

"What's going on there now?"

"Nothing."

"Looks to me like a lot of smoke."

"Smoke maybe. But no fire."

"Are you rock solid sure of it?"

Atticus nodded.

"Can I tell the President he can quit worrying about Baden-Baden?"

"The fire is out." Atticus shrugged his big shoulders. "It won't burn again."

Fuller paused and stared at the ceiling for a moment. "You're pretty well connected over there, aren't you?"

"Some people think I am."

"What's the problem between the Germans and the Jews?"

Atticus shrugged again. "It is the story, the tragedy of mankind," he said. "The Germans have what the Jews want, and the Jews have what the Germans want. They won't talk to each other, so, I'm afraid, they have to kill each other."

"The President is concerned because we have a lot of major business contracts with German companies," Fuller said.

"That concerns us all."

"He doesn't want to lose them."

"I'm confident he won't."

"A war wouldn't help any of us."

Atticus forced a wry grin. "Wars are never triggered by big incidents," he said, "only the small ones that seem insignificant at the time."

"Was there one in Baden-Baden?"

"There was."

"What's the status?"

"It lies in its own grave."

Fuller stood, picked his black overcoat up from the foot of the bed and strode toward the door.

"Don't let anybody dig it up," he said.

Atticus smiled and reached for the room menu. Samuel Fuller had not even offered him coffee.

Samuel Fuller would live to regret it.

33.

THE TRAIN BORE through the gray of a day made dark by heavy snowfall that turned the forests into shadow tunnels and erased the sky with a layer of clouds the color of dirty flannel. Ambrose glanced at the sleeping German officer on the far side of the compartment. The aging man's chin had dropped to his chest, and the drool at the corners of his mouth had turned to froth, speckled with blood.

"He won't disturb us," said the man with the bulbous nose. He pulled his overcoat tighter around his throat and his woolen hat down low over his eyes.

Ambrose Lincoln studied him closely.

The man was younger than he looked.

The years had not aged him.

But they had been hard years.

His face was weathered.

He wore a patch over his left eye, probably made from pigskin. It was scratched in places where it shouldn't be scratched at all. A ragged scar curved like the blade of a saber from the patch down to a small, pointed chin that was mostly hidden by a well-groomed goatee, black and sprinkled with a touch of gray.

His clothes had once borne fancy price tags. He was obviously a man of means.

Life meant little to him. The German officer had gone to sleep on the eastern side of Katowice. He would not awaken in Strasbourg.

He would not awaken at all.

"You know Rachel," Lincoln said.

"I do." The man's voice was filled with gravel.

"What do you know about Rachel?"

"I know you are looking for her."

"Perhaps I'm not," Lincoln said, watching the man the way a predator stares at his prey.

His muscles were tense. His nerves were on edge.

He did not know which of them was the predator.

And which was the prey.

Lincoln saw the bulge on the inside the black overcoat. It was a large pistol, an automatic no doubt. He would never be able to reach it in time.

Perhaps he did not need to. He had killed the German officer swiftly and silently, and no one had seen him, not even Ambrose Lincoln, and Lincoln made it a point to see everything.

The man with the bulbous nose smiled.

"These are very difficult times," he said. "These are the worst of times. You see the phone lines torn down, you see the telegraph wires ripped from their poles, you believe that the world is isolated and out of touch, that a great empty abyss exists between us all."

Lincoln narrowed his eyes.

There was no reason to speak.

He had nothing to say.

The man with the bulbous nose continued, "But in your heart you know that is not true. Our games are different from others, the ones you and I play. It is not our sole endeavor to win. We play to keep from losing because when we lose, we have so much to lose." He shrugged. "We knew you were coming before you knew you were coming, Mister Lincoln. Or should I say Mister Klaus?"

"Either name is fine."

"Are either one of them accurate?"

"Not that I'm away of."

"You think you are at a terrible disadvantage," the man said. "We know you. You do not know me now. You will not know me when we go our separate ways."

"What about Rachel?"

"She is in hiding."

"Do you know where?"

"Rachel has vanished."

"She has left Baden-Baden?"

"She has left period." The man reached in his pocket and retrieved a pair of leather gloves. The burnished pigskin matched his patch. He pulled them tightly on his hands. "I don't think you will find her," he said.

"Why are you looking for Rachel?" Lincoln asked.

"I'm not."

"But you have something for me."

"I do."

He pulled a small square of paper from the vest pocket of his overcoat and handed it to Lincoln.

It was an address: *2416 Eckbergstrasse*.

"It's where her father lived," the man said. "He had a photography studio there."

"But Rachel is no longer there."

"No."

"What am I to do when I find her?" Lincoln asked.

"Perhaps you were sent to save her," the man said. "Perhaps you were sent to kill her. I do not know. I presume you will in time. I had the duty of providing you with her home address. My job is finished."

"So you are not going to Baden-Baden."

"I have no reason to go any farther than Strasbourg."

Ambrose Lincoln nodded at the German officer.

"Why was it necessary to kill him?" he asked.

The man with the bulbous nose laughed out loud. "Because I could," he said, "and because he was a German."

He remained seated, staring out the window, watching a world turned white.

Lincoln left the compartment and stepped out into the snowfall. His glanced at the schedule on the wall. The train to Baden-Baden would be leaving at six o'clock. He had forty-five minutes before boarding. Lincoln found a small restaurant across the street from the station and had a plate of Schlachtschussel, an odd combination of blood and liver sausages piled atop hot kraut. He did not taste it, but it did not cost much, and it warmed him.

Ambrose Lincoln looked again at the address: *2416 Eckbergstrasse.*

Why was he given something he could easily find himself?

Who knew he was coming?

Who was the man with the bulbous nose?

Who had hired him?

Who had sent him?

And why was the German dead and he still alive?

As Ambrose Lincoln walked into the train station, he did not see the man with the bulbous nose waiting in the shadows. As soon as Lincoln moved out onto the platform, he stepped to the ticket window.

"I would like a train to Baden-Baden," he said.

"We have one leaving in five minutes," the agent said.

"I'll take the next one."

"It does not leave until midnight."

"Midnight will do."

"Name?" the agent asked.

"Leopold," the man said. "Bertram Leopold."

"Reason for your travel?"

The man with the bulbous nose smiled broadly.

"Pleasure," he said.

34.

AMBROSE LINCOLN STEPPED off the train at Baden-Baden and into the fires of a madman's personal hell. He had been the only passenger to ride to the city, and now he knew why. There was the thick aroma of burning flesh in the air. Smoke fell from the rooftops like a mist of smoldering embers. Darkened streets around the station were littered with piles of trash that had been set ablaze.

The streets were empty.

No people.

No cars.

Only the shadows.

And even the shadows looked out of place.

Lincoln was staring into the gaunt, skeletal face of a German officer, who was obviously the man in charge. His dark hair was thinning and combed across his head in an effort to hide the balding spots. It hadn't worked.

His eyes were hard.

His nose was much too large for his face.

His skin looked a sickly yellow in the pale moonlight.

The officer was frowning, slowly thumbing through a stack of papers on his clipboard. Behind him, four guards stood at attention. The barrels of their 8 mm Mauser bolt action rifles were trained on him. From a distance of ten feet, they could not miss.

Lincoln studied their eyes

The soldier on the end would kill him in a heartbeat.

The other three would hesitate.

He forgot about them.

They were no longer part of the equation or of any concern.

The German officer swaggered up on front of Lincoln. The SS insignia on his collar glistened beneath the gaslight. The letters looked like lightning bolts. The name on the chest of his uniform was Captain Konrad Emmerich.

It was a name Lincoln would not forget.

His smile was cold.

"Name," he asked.

"Wagner," Lincoln replied.

"First name?"

"Klaus."

"And you came here from Strasbourg?"

"I did."

"Alone."

"Apparently so."

"Your passport?"

Lincoln handed it to the officer.

"Jewish?" the officer said.

"No."

"Why are you here?"

"Business."

"With whom?"

"The craftsmen of Baden-Baden make excellent clocks and watches." Lincoln shrugged. "I buy their clocks and watches here and sell them somewhere else."

"Where?"

"America mostly.."

"You are an American?"

"Second generation. My mother and father came from Munich."

"They should not have left."

Lincoln shrugged "It was a matter out of my hands."

"I was expecting someone else," Emmerich said. "Colonel Dieter Ulrich was scheduled to arrive on this train."

Lincoln waited.

"Did you see him?"

"I would not know him."

"So he did not get on in Strasbourg."

"I saw no one else board the train in Strasbourg."

"That is odd," Emmerich said.

He paused and stared at the sky as the snow began to fall again. It was little more than a light sprinkling, nothing to worry about.

The Captain tried to smile.

It was pointless.

"Are you armed?" he asked Lincoln.

Ambrose Lincoln slowly removed the Luger from his belt. "For protection when I travel," he said.

Emmerich took the Luger and handed it to one of the guards. "You will be safe here," he said. "You will have no reason for a weapon."

Lincoln nodded. "Will it be returned to me when I leave?"

The Captain bowed slightly. "Most assuredly," he said. "In other parts of the world, you will not be as safe as you are in Baden-Baden."

Emmerich turned and gestured grandly toward the empty streets.

"See," he said. "you have nothing to fear in Baden-Baden."

He stepped aside, and Lincoln descended the steps to the pavement. He was facing a strange town on a strange mission under strange circumstances at a strange time in his life.

Somehow none of it seemed strange.

He may have only been walking the back alleys of his mind.

But he had been here before.

Or he had been to someplace that looked a lot like a dying Baden-Baden when the lights go out. Lincoln walked down the dark street and left the glow of the gaslight behind him. The snow against the building had melted. By morning, it would freeze again. The cold dug deep into an old wound just below the third rib on his left side. In time, the cold would end the pain as well.

Baden-Baden had become a town of silence.

No screams.

No whimpers.

It was as though the town was afraid to breathe.

Afraid to move.

Afraid.

On the platform, Captain Emmerich motioned toward the shadows. A small woman with red hair pulled by and clipped low at her neckline and wearing a black leather overcoat walked toward him. "Don't lose the American," he said. "Keep your distance, but keep you eyes on him. He will suspect one of us. He does not trust any of us. He will not suspect you. He will regard you as simply another misplaced woman who needs a little help. If he offers to help you, let him. But don't lose him. He will lead us to the girl, and she will give us the film."

"What about the American?" she asked.

"When?"

"After we find the girl."

"Don't worry about the American."

"Why not?"

"Leopold will take care of him."

"Leopold is not here."

Captain Emmerich smiled. "He will be when it's time for the American to die," he said.

Emmerich turned and walked away as the train left the station. The whistle blew, and it sounded like a cry in the night.

35.

IT WOULD HAVE been difficult for Liese Himmel to hide in either the shadows or a crowd, remain discreet, or appear anonymous. She was almost six feet tall, had the long slender legs of a ballet dancer, and a flash of red streaks in her auburn hair. It was an accident of birth and nothing else. Her smile was genuine when she smiled, but it was seldom.

Her back bore deep scars left by the whip of her first husband. He was an artist, a tortured soul, forever chased by footsteps in the dark, a bag of skin packed tight with fear and paranoia. Fritz freed himself of the torment burning his soul by beating his wife, and once he was free of his demons, he would lay his head in her naked lap and cry, begging her forgiveness while the blood spilled from the cuts and soaked into the wooden pine floors.

Fritz had already cried himself to sleep on an April morning in 1935 when she placed the barrel of a shotgun against his head and pulled the trigger. Liese did what he had been unable to do. No longer was there a burning torment in his soul. She had freed him.

She looked to see if there was gratitude in his eyes.

The eyes were gone.

Liese Himmel walked eight blocks naked through the town of Hellersdorf, carrying the shotgun.

Her jaws were clenched.

Her face was stoic.

The blood was drying on her back.

She walked into the polizeistation, placed the shotgun on the counter and said, "My husband is dead."

The police chief took one look at her and said he would handle such a delicate and sensitive situation personally.

He waited for Liese to smile.

She didn't.

Basil Gloeckner, whose position had turned him from a street cop to a man of means, drove her to his home on the edge of the garden district, gently washed the blood from her back with warm water, covered the raw scars with a poultice, and bathed her with spice and oils.

The chief put Liese to bed, and because he was a man and all women needed a man, crawled beneath the flannel sheets with her.

The next morning, Fritz Himmel was officially charged and convicted of assault on a woman and buried without the trappings of a funeral. There were no prayers or scriptural dissertation over his remains. No preacher had sought to pave his way to heaven. It was just as well. Fritz Himmel had already met his maker face to face without a counselor to defend his worthless soul.

On Thursday afternoon, the police chief left work early.

Liese was waiting for him.

On Friday, he did not come to the station at all.

And no one dared disturb him.

On Monday morning, shortly after ten-thirty, the body of Basil Gloeckner was found on the floor of his bedroom with a kitchen butcher knife shoved into his chest. *It probably struck his heart* was the investigating officer's first opinion.

He had been dead for three days.

Liese Himmel was nowhere to be found.

She had left her clothes.

She had left her purse.

It was empty.

It was as though Liese Himmel had walked to the edge of Hellersdorf and stepped off the edge of the world.

She had.

The snow had become much heavier during the past thirty minutes and was piling up on the frozen streets of Baden-Baden. The light from kerosene lanterns flickered nervously throughout the neighborhood. It spilled from the windows but could not penetrate the darkness.

One thing quickly became obvious to Liese.

The American had no idea where he was going. He walked up one street and down the next, pausing only long enough to check the signs above each intersection. Two lovers passed him arm-in-arm. He had not noticed them. A taxi driver pulled to the curb and tried to find a fare. The American kept walking.

Ambrose Lincoln stopped beside a small café, stared through the door for a moment, and then walked in. An older couple was drinking wine in the back. Two businessmen sat beside the front window, lost in conversation. The window had become coated with frost. A radio was playing somewhere, probably the kitchen. American jazz. Some kid piano player named Fats Waller. The song sounded so familiar. Lincoln had never heard it before.

He found a table where he could sit with his back to the wall and eased into the chair. Time and age were catching up to him.

A man who lost a night of sleep aged a week. A man who lost two nights of sleep would find his rest in a grave.

He had no idea who had told him that.

But the voice was harsh.

And brittle.

He ordered coffee.

"You won't be able to sleep," the aging waitress said.

"I hope not."

"You will like the beef and bean stew," she said.

"Do you have eggs?"'

She nodded.

"Three eggs," he said. "Mashed flat and fried well done."

As she walked away, Lincoln saw a tall blonde walk into the café. Her hair looked red in the dim light,

A temptress, he thought.

A seductress.

Liese Himmel looked at him and smiled.

There was no doubt left in his mind.

She had not come to spend the night with him.

She had come to kill him.

Beautiful women, especially those with long legs and red hair, only had one reason to lay their slender and naked bodies across Ambrose Lincoln's chest as the dark of the night closed in like a noose around them,

They wanted him dead.

He smiled to himself.

Would she fire the bullet? Or would she merely keep him occupied while another took his life?

Liese Himmel sat down beside him.

Her smile seemed to say that she knew something he didn't. He shrugged. Everyone did.

Her scent was the fragrance of spring flowers and red wine.

He might not see morning, Lincoln thought, *but it was going to be a helluva way to die.*

36.

SHE HAD MADE the first move. Ambrose Lincoln was content to let her speak first as well. He was immediately suspicious when a woman so young and beautiful was walking in the dead of night across a section of a town that lay in shambles. He was suspicious because she was wearing a high-dollar black leather overcoat. He was suspicious because he had noticed a sag in the pocket of the coat, and it looked as though she might be carrying something heavier than lipstick. He assumed it was a pistol, small caliber, deadly at close range, and she was obviously quite talented at being able to move into close range. Long legs and a smile usually did the trick. But mostly, Lincoln was suspicious because she had walked out of the cold darkness and into his life, sitting down uninvited beside a man whose soul was as dead and empty as the streets outside.

"I saw you leave the train," she said.

Lincoln nodded.

He had not seen her.

And that troubled him.

He took a sip of his coffee, black. It was bitter. "Can I buy you something to eat?" he asked.

"No."

"I'm having eggs," he said.

She smiled.

Lincoln had always wondered what his last meal might be. He never thought it would be eggs, mashed and fried.

"I have no room for the night," she said.

"That makes two of us."

"But you can afford a room," she said.

"Usually I sleep on the streets," he said.

"That can be dangerous," she said.

"So can hotels."

She shrugged and held out her hand. "My name is Liese."

Lincoln took her hand and squeezed it. It was as soft as her voice. She seemed in no hurry to remove her hand. He let it go.

"It's a pretty name," he said.

"Do you have a name?"

He smiled again. "Several," he said.

"And what name are you using tonight?"

"I'm not," he said.

"But you have a passport."

"It's a piece of paper," he said. "Paper is a notorious liar."

"What if the authorities find out?" she asked.

"They won't," he said. "Unless you tell them."

"And why should I do that?"

"These are not the best of times," Lincoln said. "I've seen the town, but only a glimpse, and a glimpse is enough to tell me that part of Baden-Baden is dead and the rest of it is dying. Why, I have no idea. But I do know that information in a town like this is the most valuable commodity anyone can sell."

Liese sat back in her chair and studied him.

Too big.

Too old.

Too ugly.

Too tired.

Too rumpled.

Why was anyone afraid of him?

Why did anyone think he had the ability to find the missing girl when German patrols had looked all over the city for three days and had failed?

Who was he?

And what had he done?

What was he capable of doing?

Liese looked into his eyes, and then she understood.

He was not afraid to die.

She could shoot him where he sat, and he would not care. But then, he would not die alone.

He would take her with him.

She smiled. On the list of things she did best, the smile was third.

"I am not a seller of information. I am not unlike you."

"Why would you say that?" he asked.

"I am a stranger in town, too. I don't know anyone." She shrugged. "I am alone, and I don't like to be alone."

"I prefer my own company."

"I don't like to sleep alone."

"I like to wake up in the morning."

She arched an eyebrow.

The door opened, and Ambrose Lincoln watched a man move inside from the cold. Short. Overweight. Probably fifty but he looked ten years older. Whiskers. He had not shaved in days. He was not wearing a coat. He shivered as he looked around the room and brushed the snow from his sleeves. He walked toward Lincoln's table with a limp.

"I apologize for bothering you," he said, removing his cap.

"It's fine," Lincoln said.

The man reached inside his pants pocket and removed a wrinkled envelope. It was wet and smudged with mud. "Are you Mister Wagner?" he asked.

"Sometimes."

"I have your room key," he said.

"For tonight?"

"Until they burn the hotel down," he said. "The name is on the key." Lincoln nodded as the man turned abruptly and limped toward the door. He was obviously in a hurry to leave.

Liese cocked her head and placed her hand beneath her chin. "Now you won't have to sleep on the streets tonight. You have a place for both of us," she said. "You know you're not the kind of man who would leave me out in the cold."

She laughed softly.

Ambrose Lincoln's eyes lingered on her over one last time.

Tall.

Young.

Long legs.

Long, slender legs.

And beautiful.

He thought that girls who looked like she did only lived in magazines. Lincoln sighed heavily. *It would indeed be a lovely way to die*, he thought. *But not tonight*.

He stood without a word and left her sitting at the table alone.

If she did not shoot him before he reached the door, it would have been a good night.

37.

THE NAME ON the key said Rastatt Gasthaus on Wederstrasse.
Ambrose Lincoln was able to make out the names on the street signs,
at least those that still existed, by the light of the dying flames that
still licked out the broken windows of a town left deserted by the
unfortunates, the Jews, who had been dragged from its doorways and
piled on trains or in common graves.

The silence was pervasive.

The only sounds Lincoln could hear were the crackling of burning
timbers and his own footsteps.

He was the only creature, living or dead, on the streets.

It was an easy assumption to make, but he knew it was a lie that
dead men told themselves while waiting for a bullet they never
expected.

She was back there in the shadows somewhere, watching him,
waiting for him to provide her with the information she needed or
waiting for him to make a final mistake.

Liese was as patient as she was beautiful.

It grieved him to know that he would have to kill her, but it was
his only chance of staying alive.

At the moment, he could not hear her.

But he knew she was there.

He had listened for footsteps most of his life.

Hers were no different.

Lincoln found the Rastatt Gasthaus at two-seventeen in the morning if the clock out front was correct.

It wasn't.

It had not run in days.

It had not run since the gasthaus burned.

He walked into the lobby, and it smelled of smoke and charred embers. Chairs were overturned. The desk had been butchered, probably with an axe.

The concierge lay beside the elevator door. It was open.

Lincoln knelt down and closed his eyes.

What had they witnessed? What fear had they possessed?

Were the concierge and those like him the reason why he had been dispatched to Baden-Baden? Who had sent him?

And who was Rachel Gruner? Was she still alive?

What would she tell him? Or give him?

And was the beautiful, long-legged girl lagging in the shadows behind him looking for Rachel Gruner, too. If so, Liese had already dug two graves beside the streets of Baden-Baden, and she did not plan to occupy either one of them.

Ambrose Lincoln turned and stared out the broken window in the front of the gasthaus.

He saw the darkness.

Nothing else.

The darkness carried many shadows. Most would be gone at daylight.

One carried a gun.

Was she alone? He doubted it.

He looked at the key again, and in the pale light of the flames he read the room number: five-thirty-five. In the distance, he heard the low rumble of a truck growling its way down the street.

They would not be coming for him.

Those who came for him walked on cat's feet.

Soft.

And silent.

Lincoln took his time moving up the staircase to the fifth floor. Each plank was threatening to snap with every step he took. The stairs were held together by splinters. The smoke from smoldering mattresses spilled down on top of him. It was suffocating. His eyes watered. His lungs burned. But then, he had spent the night in hell before.

He eased down the hallway to room five-thirty-five. The brass numbers hung loose and crooked. He stood in front of the door, listening for any faint sounds that might be stirring inside the room.

Nothing.

Lincoln slipped the 9 mm automatic pistol from his boot and gently pushed on the door.

It was locked. He tried the key. The door creaked in frustration as it opened.

A slender shaft of moonlight fell through the broken window.

No sound.

No movement.

The room was empty. Ambrose Lincoln hated empty rooms. They could be deadly.

When the room you enter is empty, it sometimes only seems to be empty, and you're never aware you're not alone until they come to carry you to the morgue.

There was that voice again, speaking somewhere on the backside of his mind.

Harsh.

And brittle.

The desk had been ripped apart, its drawers thrown across the floor. The glass from a broken lamp lay beside the broken glass from the window. The bed had been shoved into the corner, and the stuffed cotton batting in the mattress was doing its best in cramped quarters to burn.

Lincoln lay on the floor and pushed himself up under the edge of the bed. His hands moved from one slat to the next. Wedged between the fifth slat and the springs, he touched the book.

It had not been in the desk. The desk was ruined.

If someone had not already stolen it, he knew that the Bible would be hidden beneath the bed. On the fifth floor, it would be tied to the fifth slat. He had learned it so long ago but could not remember the man who taught him, the man with a harsh voice, a brittle voice.

Room five-three-five.

Lincoln opened the Bible to the fifth book in the Bible, Deuteronomy, turned to the third chapter and read the first line of the fifth verse.

All these cities were fenced with high walls, gates, and bars.

It wasn't much. It was enough. He dropped the Bible on the floor and knew the flames would consume it before the week had ended.

Lincoln crept back down the stairs, walked past the concierge who had seen far too much on the last day of his life, and stood silently in the doorway.

The moon was playing tricks, bouncing between the street and the clouds.

A moment of light.

Then it was gone.

But all it took was a moment.

Ambrose Lincoln caught a faint glimpse of the tall, long-legged Liese, pressed tightly against the edge of an alleyway across the street. It was a snapshot in time. A single exposure. A blurred image. And then the darkness erased her again.

She was not alone.

38.

THE BROKEN THREADS of moonlight lay as splintered as the shards of glass on the streets. In the distance, flames were still spitting from the upstairs windows of little shops that surrounded the synagogue. But the screams had died away. Perhaps there was no one left to scream. The night already seemed far too dark and far too long. Liese Himmel did not trust the dark. Not all of the shadows were dead.

She had been walking three blocks behind him, across the street and standing in the doorway of a deserted bakeshop when she watched Ambrose Lincoln enter the charred remains of the gasthaus. She waited for him to reappear. She was still waiting. Liese glanced at her watch in the dim light of the moon. In twelve minutes, the time in Baden-Baden would be two o'clock. It had been almost an hour since he disappeared into a restless column of white smoke that was pouring from of the lobby. Lincoln had not come back out.

There was no sign of movement inside the gasthaus. No sounds. No sight of Ambrose Lincoln. Nothing but white smoke seducing the darkness.

"We have lost him." The voice came from behind her. She knew the man well. She had never been able to recognize the accent.

"No," she said.

"He must have gone out the back way."

"No," Liese said. "He is searching for something."

"Why do you say that?"

"He was given a key to the hotel." Liese shrugged and shivered slightly as a gust of cold wind blew the falling snow in her face. "He thought it was a room for the night," he said.

"And you offered to come with him."

"I did."

"And he rejected you."

Liese shrugged again.

"They say he's crazy," the voice said.

"Who are they?"

"The ones who removed his mind in Poland." The voice laughed. "They broke it in little pieces, and he does not know it is broken."

"He knows more than they think."

"Is he here in Baden-Baden?"

"Yes."

"Does he know why he's here?"

"Apparently he doesn't."

"Is he spending the night in a burning building?"

"Apparently he is."

"Did he turn down the opportunity to sleep with a beautiful woman?"

"He turned down the opportunity to sleep with me."

The voice laughed again, louder this time. "He is definitely crazy," the man said.

Liese stepped back in the shadows and stared into the face of Bertram Leopold. His woolen hat was pulled low on his head. The moonlight touched the ragged scar on his face. He wore his patch with a certain amount of dignity, she thought. Liese wondered how he had lost the eye, or if he had lost it at all.

She never asked.

Leopold had as many secrets as she did.

The headlights of a car, probing the snow, penetrating the darkness, coming down the street startled them. Leopold reached for his Walther P38. He eased it out of the pocket of his woolen overcoat. Liese tightened the grip on her Sauer 38H semi-automatic pistol. She and Leopold had the advantage, she thought. They had seen the car coming, and no one inside the car knew where they were hiding.

The car eased across the ice and stopped beside the curb. A Mercedes 540K. The color of night. The passenger door opened.

A man stepped out, wearing a heavy navy blue coat over a gray suit. His hair was black, So was his mustache. He was stocky with broad shoulders. He adjusted his wire-frame glasses and looked down both sides of the street before walking quickly toward the alley.

"Leopold," he said.

Silence.

"I have brought the dampftnudel," he said.

Leopold moved from the shadows. "Your accent is terrible," he said.

The American shrugged. "It's not a word we use often in New Jersey," he said. He paused. "Do you know where the target is?"

"We do."

"We?"

Liese, still clutching her pistol, eased up behind him.

"Don't move too quickly," Leopold said. "She will definitely kill you." He paused and laughed softly. "She will be disappointed if she doesn't have the opportunity."

"I thought you were working alone," the American said.

"I am working for you," Leopold said. "She is working for Captain Emmerich of the German Gestapo." He shrugged and gestured grandly. "We are together, but are each working alone."

"The same objective, I presume."

"You don't want the photographs of the Night of Broken Glass to show up in America because you can't afford to stir up any raw emotions that might persuade the Americans to go to war with Germany."

"You are correct."

"And the Germans don't want to fight the Americans either," Leopold said. "The Night of Broken Glass was nothing more than a simple protest that got out of hand. Some died. Some have been removed to prison camps. The Germans, too, fear that the photographs may inflame the anger among some in America. The Germans have no interest in creating an incident that may create a conflict with your business and your President."

"The President would just as soon the photographs be erased."

"And the photographer?"

"Erased as well."

"Let sleeping dogs lie is, I believe, the phrase you Americans like to use," Leopold said.

"It is an appropriate phrase to use here." He turned to face Liese.

The barrel of the Sauer 38H was jammed between his eyes.

"How did you know where we were?" she demanded, speaking softly through clenched teeth.

"We have our ways."

"That is not good enough."

"Leopold is our man," the American said. "He makes sure we are kept informed. We pay him quite well for that."

Liese turned and jammed the pistol in Leopold's face.

"You have betrayed me," she said.

Leopold thought she would pull the trigger.

She didn't.

He took a breath.

"What can I tell the President?" the American said as he climbed back into the Mercedes.

"Tell him everything will be erased."

Liese had not moved. The pistol had not wavered.

She could kill Leopold as far as the American was concerned. He felt quite confident that she would be able to eliminate the problem with or without his man being involved. He pulled a leather notebook from his suit pocket and began looking through an alphabetical list of names in Europe in case Leopold had to be replaced.

39.

AMBROSE LINCOLN HAD found a small anteroom on the eastern side of the old gasthaus that had not yet been touched by the flames or suffocated by the smoke. He turned an overstuffed chair toward the wall, sat down, and closed his eyes. In the darkness, he could not be seen by anyone who walked through the door on the far side of the room. He only hoped that he would be able to hear them coming before they made their way through the ruins scattered about the lobby. His arm lay across his chest, clutching the Heckler & Koch 9 mm pistol. Time for him had stopped. There was daylight and dark, and he was caught somewhere in between.

A heavy snow was piling up on the sill of the broken window. A stiff wind whistled into the anteroom. Lincoln was cold. It was a good feeling. When he felt nothing at all, he figured, it would be time for concern.

He closed his eyes and slept.

But not as well as the concierge.

By morning, one of them would wake up.

Then again, maybe not.

It was still dark when Ambrose Lincoln realized that he was still among the living. He wondered what had startled him. He listened for a sound. Nothing. He listened for footsteps. Nothing. All he heard was the sound of his own breathing. He wasn't disappointed.

A sharp crack.

It reverberated just outside the door of the anteroom, and he wasn't nearly as cold as he had been. The side of his face felt as though it had been scorched, and Lincoln could see the flames growing larger and out of control as they spread down the hall and began chewing through the walls around him.

The timbers were crackling.

The smoke was coming in waves.

The ceiling was falling as strips of burning embers, and the gusts of cold wind only served to feed it.

Lincoln glanced around and realized he had a single avenue of escape, and death might be waiting on the other side. He wondered if Liese's pistol was trained on the window, and if a woman so soft and beautiful was hard enough and tough enough to pull the trigger.

He suspected she was.

Lincoln moved quickly to the window and used his elbow to break away the splintered glass remaining in the frame. The alley outside was narrow and banked with snow. A faint crease of morning had broken like a slender thread of light in the distance.

The fire was on a rampage now. It had devoured the table and was marching toward the chair. Lincoln climbed through the window, dropped to the pavement, and into the snow. He knelt and raised his pistol, squinting as he tried to focus with a stinging blizzard hammering his face.

He waited for the bullets.

No one stepped into the far end of the alley.

No one fired.

The morning had broken in silence. It stayed that way.

He was still alive. Liese must want him that way.

He had no idea who might have joined her.

Her boss?

An aide?

A stranger?

He doubted if Liese had a boss. She no doubt received orders. Her financial payments came from someone. She may have known who hired her. Then again, she might not care. Her gun simply belonged to the highest bidder.

She had a talent for finding the target, and Liese was, he suspected, the kind of mercenary who worked alone.

So much for having an aide.

So whose shadow had he seen with her?

And did that shadow still exist?

Or was the shadow from the night before walking with the concierge across a land from which they could not return?

Lincoln eased down the narrow passageway toward the back of the alley. He rounded the corner and walked alone down an empty street. A light came on in a window above him. An old lady was dragging a bag of trash toward the curb. A child stood in the doorway of a fire-ravaged building. A young woman in a yellow dress was sweeping broken glass away from her shop.

The old man, the child, the lady in the yellow dress all had one thing in common. None of them was smiling.

Ambrose Lincoln knew what he was looking for. The first line of the fifth verse in the third chapter of Deuteronomy had told him: *All these cities were fenced with high walls, gates, and bars.*

It might be a home.

It might be a shop.

It might be a gasthaus.

He didn't know for sure.

But Lincoln knew he would recognize the place when he saw it.

The Jewish section of Baden-Baden no longer had even the faint resemblance of a town. It was a skeleton with bones of brick and charred timbers, a grotesque landscape of hell created by an artistic madman in a world of smoke and snow painted black and white.

He had been walking for hours when he saw the stained gray building on the edge of town, barely visible in a heavy snowfall that showed no intention of letting up. The sign had been torn down and propped against a wrought iron gate. Once it had been a clinic, a refuge for comfort and sometimes healing. Now it looked like the final resting place for the damned.

The gate hung crookedly from a crumbling rock wall that rose for two stories and wrapped itself around the decaying structure. It reeked with the silence and the stench of death. Lincoln could see no flicker of light or any traces of life inside. Iron bars formed a grill across the windows.

Ambrose Lincoln had no idea where he was, but he saw *the fence, the gate, and the bars* and knew he was in the right place.

The door was cracked. He opened it and walked in. The lobby of the clinic, even in the dim light, looked no different from the gasthaus. It was in total disarray. The windows were broken. The furniture had been ripped apart. The reason for the damage made no sense at all.

There were bloodstains on the floor.

The fires had died away and the charred ruins turned cold.

Snow lay upon the embers.

Lincoln took the stairway to the basement, and there, hiding in the shadows he found the huddled masses, or at least what were left of them.

Vacant eyes.

Empty faces.

Lives in shambles.

An American stood and adjusted his glasses. He was stooped and gaunt, and a week's worth of whiskers masked his pallid face. He was wearing khakis – shirt and trousers. His eyes were on the verge of desperation. They softened.

"Lincoln?" he said.

Lincoln nodded.

"I knew you would come," he said.

He held out his hand. Lincoln took hold of it. The man's hands were trembling.

"Priestly," he said. "Robert Priestly."

"I thought you were dead."

The American grinned. "I probably am," he said.

40.

AMBROSE LINCOLN QUICKLY surveyed the room. Two matronly old women, obviously grieving, and an aging man were lying on cots. They had no doubt been confined to the clinic when the attacks came. The oldest of the women was crying. The other was staring out the window. She was shivering. The chill had burrowed its way into her bones. The old man slept.

In the corner sat a family of three, desperately holding on to each other. Lives full of promise. Lives changed in an instant. Lives changed when the guns fired and the screaming began. Lives changed when the glass broke.

The little girl was barely three, and any hope she had of reaching four was dying with every passing hour. A young woman had pushed herself beneath the desk. She was wearing a dark blue dress with faded green flowers. Her alabaster face was drawn and devoid of any makeup. Her ebony hair fell raggedly on her shoulders. Her eyes were those of a rabbit watching the hawk drop from the sky. She must run, but there was nowhere to run. You wait. And you die. And that is life.

Priestly sat back down on the floor and leaned against the wall. He looked up at Lincoln. "I assume you don't know why you're here?"

"You are correct."

"No one ever tells you."

"It's the way you keep secrets."

"And if I wasn't here?"

"It would always be a secret."

Priestly nodded.

"You were given a name."

"Rachel Gruner."

Priestly nodded toward the girl huddled back beneath the desk. "Meet Rachel Gruner," he said.

She did her best to smile.

Lincoln smiled back.

Rachel looked away.

He was her hope.

And he was a shell of man.

"I'm Ambrose Lincoln," he said.

Rachel glanced up.

"I am waiting for Klaus Wagner."

Lincoln shrugged. "I am also Klaus Wagner."

He thought she might cry.

"You understand the problem here," Priestly said.

"It's a puzzle with a lot of pieces missing," Lincoln answered. "I'll try to fill them in."

Lincoln nodded.

"Are you taking notes?"

"I'll remember."

"I was told your mind played tricks sometimes."

Lincoln grinned. "They believe what they want to believe."

"So you're not crazy."

"I found you."

This time Priestly grinned.

"Only a crazy man would try." Priestly grew serious. He coughed, and his throat had a rattle. He and Lincoln both knew what it meant. It no longer was a concern to either of them.

"The Germans want to eliminate the Jews," he said.

"It's been rumored."

"It's more than a rumor." Priestly coughed again. "Their final solution is taking place all over Austria and Germany," he said. "They began in Baden-Baden."

"The newspapers say it was a protest."

"The newspapers are lying."

"The President's people say a bunch of angry vandals came in, broke a few windows, set a few shops on fire, and German soldiers finally brought everything under control and hauled them away."

"Does it look that way to you?"

"No."

"The President's people are lying."

Lincoln glimpsed a movement out of the corner of his eye. He looked over his shoulder and caught the faint image of a woman walking quietly into the room. Lincoln's eyes fell on the small, oval face of a young woman, maybe thirty, maybe not, with long raven hair and a beauty mark or a spot of mud under her left eye. She was barely five feet tall and wore a woolen dress the color of the earth. Her skin was pale, translucent, and had not yet been touched by the sun. She was barefoot and carrying a bleached cotton sack. Her eyes were dark, filled with bitterness and regret.

He had seen her before.

She, too, had told him about the lies. She smiled her sad smile and sat with the family. Maybe she had come for them – to take them with her. Maybe she had come for him.

She would someday.

He had no doubt about it.

"Rachel can prove it is all a lie," Priestly said. "Her father was a photographer. He captured the whole damn thing on film. The Germans don't want the people in America to see them. There are some in the government who don't want America to see them. There are a lot in big business that don't want America to see them."

"Why?"

"When you see the photographs you'll understand." Priestly shrugged his weary shoulders. "They'll make you sick," he said. "They'll make you mad. You'll see what's happening behind the big lie. Americans don't like to be lied to."

"And I'm supposed to bring the bad news home."

"You're supposed to bring the bad news, the film, and the girl home."

"Why the girl?"

"Otherwise, she's dead."

Priestly stood and counted ten bricks down from the top of the room and fifteen bricks to the left. He loosened the brick, pulled it out, and removed a folder. He handed it to Lincoln.

It held four photographs.

An old man was on his knees, obviously begging for his life, when the German soldier shot him.

A boy had been pushed against a stone wall. His sister lay dead at his feet. He had been crying. The tears were still on his face when the shots were fired.

A family of four were kneeling on broken glass in front of their shop. A German officer stood behind the man with a Luger jammed against the back of his head, and the man's head was exploding.

A woman was holding her child tightly, her eyes wide with confusion and fright.

He had seen the woman before and again. He gazed down on the small, oval face of a young woman, maybe thirty, maybe not, with long raven hair and a beauty mark or a spot of mud under her left eye. She was barely five feet tall and wore a woolen dress the color of the earth. Her skin was pale, translucent, and had not yet been touched by the sun. She was barefoot and carrying a bleached cotton sack. Her eyes were dark, filled with bitterness and regret.

He looked up and searched the room for the woman.

She was gone.

"Can you do it?" Priestly asked.

Lincoln nodded and reached for Rachel's hand.

She smiled.

Robert Priestly was dead before any of them heard the shot. His body was thrown against the wall, his eyes open wide with amazement, and a small hole had appeared just below the hairline.

Lincoln threw himself on top of Rachel and waited for the sniper to fire again.

41.

HE LAY IN silence, the sound of death, but only for an instant. Ambrose Lincoln could feel Rachel trembling beneath him. It was the tremble of the condemned who knows the gallows have been built, the hanging rope purchased, and the footsteps echoing down the dark hallways belong to a priest coming one last time to save a lost and wretched soul.

Lincoln glanced around him and made the decision quickly. Robert Priestly could be forgotten. He had already used up his final moments on earth. He no longer had to wait for death. It found him just as the night ended, the sun rose above the fresh snows of a gray city, and the shadows had been diverted into other places. The bullet had bored a small hole above his eye and removed the back of his head.

He was one of the fortunate.

People were afraid to die because they were afraid of the great unknown. The act of dying was simple. One breath came never to be followed by another. Robert Priestly had died before he realized that death was tracking him down. None of them heard the shot that shattered the last fragments of glass in a small, bare window just above ground level.

A sniper, no doubt.

He had waited all night.

Patient.

Cold.

Content to wait.

Or had he followed Lincoln to the clinic?

Had he fired the kill shot and moved on?

Or was he still out there?

Waiting.

Watching.

The shootist was in no hurry.

He had all day or the rest of his life.

The shootist had made the first move.

The next one belonged to Lincoln.

Check.

Check mate.

One of the old women on the cot was clutching her Torah. She knew the end was near. The other lay sleeping. Maybe it was the final sleep. She coughed. She had not left them yet, but there was no food, no water to drink, no heat, only a pervasive cold that had worked itself into their bone marrow. No. She had not left them yet, but she would not stay much longer. The old man was chanting. The family was huddled together, arms wrapped around each other, lambs ready for the slaughter.

Lincoln had fought this kind of war before.

The living in the room had one chance to survive.

He must find an avenue to get out as quickly as possible.

The Germans, perhaps, would leave them all alone if he weren't with them.

Priestly was gone.

He was the last target.

He and a Jewish girl named Rachel.

Lincoln crouched low, reached over, and removed a Smith and Browning HP from Priestly's belt and shoved it into his own. He slowly turned the big, wooden desk on its side and pushed Rachel behind it. It was as good a place as any to hide, if only for a moment, and a moment might be all he needed.

He put a finger to his lips and motioned for the family to remain quiet. The old man kept chanting. It was too late to silence him. He would go out with a prayer on his lips.

Maybe it was better that way.

Lincoln could hear footsteps and muffled voices above them in the lobby. There were two of them. Maybe three.

He opened the folder and removed the four damning photographs, scattering them haphazardly on the floor in front of the desk. Lincoln took a handful of Robert Priestly's blood and bathed his face, then splashed it on his shirt. A chill worked its way through the basement. The blood was still warm.

Lincoln lay back, slumped against the wall.

And waited.

He was no different from the sniper.

He was in no hurry.

He had all day or the rest of his life.

The footsteps reached the top of the staircase that led into the basement. The voices were louder now. One cursed. And one laughed.

The laughter sounded familiar.

The single beam of a powerful flashlight cut through the darkness of the early morning. The German point man followed it downward, taking one cautious step at a time. He was clutching a Luger, his eyes trying to dart in all directions at once. He was little more than a boy, a boy with a helmet, a gun, and a flashlight.

A man in a heavy woolen coat pushed the soldier aside and stepped into the basement. A woolen hat was pulled low over his side. He carried his pistol loosely in his right hand, and it dangled beside his leg.

Ambrose Lincoln recognized him immediately: the man from the train, the man who called himself Leopold, the man who had walked away from him in Strasbourg, the man who said he had no reason to come to Baden-Baden.

His smile was a smirk. He glanced around the room and knew immediately that his work was done.

A German Gestapo officer stepped into the room.

"Are they Americans here?" he asked.

"Dead."

"Both of them?"

Leopold nodded.

"What shall we do with them?"

"They will, of course, be reported as missing." Leopold shrugged. "As far as the government is concerned, they did not exist and were never here."

"Good."

"The rest, Colonel, belong to you," Leopold said. He grinned. "I've only come for the photographs."

He knelt and began picking them up, one at a time, stopping to study each image. He shook his head.

"What will you do with them?" the colonel asked.

Leopold did not answer him. He reached into his coat pocket and removed a cigarette lighter. He set each photograph ablaze, holding it as long as he dared and watching the glossy images turn to blackened ash.

It was a ritual.

He was mesmerized.

He was still watching the flame when the bullet tore through his head.

Ambrose Lincoln fired once.

Then again.

The Gestapo colonel was dead before he hit the floor.

The young soldier was mesmerized.

He stood motionless. He was nothing but a boy fighting a mad man's war, a boy who should be home with his mother, maybe milking a cow at first dawn or walking with his father to the fields.

The boy raised his pistol. He did not know what else to do. It was too late to run.

"I am so sorry," Lincoln whispered.

The bullet caught the soldier just below his chin. He fell gagging to the floor, clawing at his throat. One last shot, and the basement was silent.

Even the chanting had stopped.

42.

AMBROSE LINCOLN PUSHED the desk aside and helped Rachel
Gruner to her feet. Her eyes swept the floor.

Too much blood.

Too much death.

She shuddered.

"Are you hurt?" he asked.

"No."

"Are you all right?"

"No."

All color had drained from her face.

The basement was in a deep chill, and a strong wind was pushing
snowflakes through the broken widow. Her hair was wet with sweat
that only fear could squeeze from her body, and it was plastered to
her face. She was shivering.

"My father is dead," she said. Her voice cracked. "My home is
gone. My friends are gone. My synagogue is gone. My school is gone.
Only God in heaven knows what has happened to my students. The
old people have been murdered and their bodies burned. The young
women have been raped and thrown away like garbage. Young men
have been taken to work camps. They will work until they die. They
may not have to work long. The children are on the street like stray
dogs, searching for their mamas, and their mamas are only a memory,

and the memories are already fading, and no one sings them to sleep anymore." She shook her head and turned away.

"No," she said again, "No one is all right here. No one will ever be all right again."

"I need the film," he said.

"You allowed him to burn the photographs."

"I gambled that you have the film," he said.

"And that's why I am alive."

"It is," he said.

Rachel walked to the cot on the far side of the basement and held an old woman's hand. "She's dead," Rachel said to no one in particular.

"I thought she would be."

"You did not save her."

"She could not be saved."

"How do you know?"

"Death settled in her eyes long before you and I got here."

Rachel patted her hand and moved to the old man's cot. His eyes were closed, and he was chanting again.

"Will you save him?"

"That job belongs to a higher power," Lincoln said.

He knelt beside the family, still holding on to each other. "We are leaving," he said. "You can go with us."

"Where are you going?"

"I don't know."

"We are dead if they find us on the streets," the man said.

"You are dead if they find you here."

The man shrugged.

"This, too, shall pass," the woman said. "We are safe here. We have a roof over our head. We have shelter from the cold."

Lincoln let his gaze strike the faces of Leopold, the Gestapo officer, and a boy soldier who had picked the wrong day to die.

"You are here among the dead," he said.

"When night comes," the man said. "I will remove them."

"And what will you do about food?"

"I will be like the Germans."

His laugh was a sneer. "I will steal."

The mother tilted his chin, and her eyes were filled with defiance. "These struggles are not new to us," she said. "We have suffered before. For generations we have suffered. For centuries, our people have endured. It has been worse. It will be worse again. We will prevail."

The little girl was crying

She wasn't afraid.

She was hungry.

The man reached up and shook Lincoln's hand. "I cannot fight your kind of wars," he said.

Lincoln stood.

"Godspeed," the man said.

Lincoln smiled. It was a lie.

He reached down and removed Leopold's heavy woolen overcoat. He no longer had any use for it. He wrapped the coat around Rachel's frail shoulders.

"Thank you," she whispered.

Even beneath the overcoat she was shivering.

It wasn't the cold.

"Do you have the film" he asked.

"It's not here."

"I didn't think it would be."

"Why should I give you the film?" she said.

Lincoln shrugged. "I have a feeling that your father did not take the pictures for his scrapbook," he said. "He took them for a reason. Only you know what that reason is. My job is to make sure the Americans understand what took place here."

"Why?"

"That was the job I was given," he said quietly.

"I don't believe you."

Lincoln grinned. "Most people don't," he said.

"Why would you risk your life for a handful of pictures?"

"Somebody somewhere thinks they are important."

"And what do you believe?" Rachel asked as she folded her arms in defiance. He could hear the tears in her voice.

43.

THE SUN WAS doing its best to warm the streets of Baden-Baden, but Liese Himmel remained back in the shadows, out of the wind and in the cold. Her eyes remained firmly fixed on the front door of the clinic. She had lived inside the dark corners for so long that she found a calm familiarity and comfort within them.

She heard Captain Emmerich and his troops walking down the alley behind her, their boots scraping the broken glass that lay hidden beneath a shallow coating of snow. She had expected him earlier. Her grip tightened on the Sauer 38H.

Liese had found the target. He, the girl, and film were trapped.

In the eyes of the Gestapo, Liese knew, she was no longer needed. One more casualty on the streets of Baden-Baden wouldn't make any difference to them or the Reich. She glanced around, her lips tight, her eyes glaring at him.

The captain was wearing a strange little smile.

She had seen it before. It was the smile he wore when he knew someone was about to die.

"You have found the girl?" he said.

"The American did."

"So you have found the film."

"Only if she has it with her."

"That's of little consequence," the captain said.

"What makes you say that?"

"She knows where the film is."

"I'm sure she hid it."

"Then she will tell me where it is."

"She will die first."

"She may not be like you, Liese," the captain said. "Not all women prefer to die first. Most will talk quickly. They fear the knife more than they fear death. They fear what I can do with a knife more than they fear death."

"The American will stop you."

"When the American woke up this morning, he was already dead."

"But no one told him."

Emmerich laughed. "I will tell him in person."

The captain had brought five Gestapo troopers with him. They were young. Their eyes were made of stone. They had been trained to kill and brainwashed to look forward to the assignment. They were tough. They were disciplined. They were loyal. There were those within the Reich who referred to them as machines.

The Reich, however, had forgotten one thing. The troopers had no idea they were vulnerable. The Reich had not taught them how to die or even that death was an option or a probability.

Captain Emmerich rubbed his hands together to keep them warm. He squinted as he looked into the glare of the sun rising above the clinic. "Are you alone?" he asked.

"I am."

"Where is Leopold?"

"He was impatient."

"Has he already gone into the clinic?"

"He has."

"Alone?"

"He carried one of your officers and a soldier with him."

"Colonel Fleischer?"

"It was."

"Fleischer likes the glory of it all. He always has. He gets the pictures, and, he figures, he gets the medal." The Captain laughed caustically.

"He won't be getting the medal," Liese said.

"Why not?"

"He and Leopold walked into the clinic eighty-seven minutes ago by my watch."

"And they have not come out."

"No."

"Gunshots?"

"Four of them?"

Captain Emmerich shook his head. Maybe disgust. Maybe sadness. "Fleischer was a hothead," he said. "He was also my friend."

Liese did not respond.

She had not removed her eyes from the clinic.

"Have you detected any movement inside?" the Captain asked.

"No."

"They may all be dead."

"There were five men inside the clinic and four shots," Liese said. "The sniper thinks he took out one, but it was a narrow shot. He does not know. As of yet, no one has left the clinic. Leopold and the colonel would have walked out by now. If anyone is alive, it's the American, and he can wait till dark."

"I won't wait that long."

Liese shrugged. A small smile tugged at the corner of her mouth. It was a smile of pity. She leaned against the face of the brick building and watched Captain Emmerich and his troopers march doggedly across the street. They had the same mind-set that possessed Leopold. They would take the American by force.

He could beat one or maybe two of them.

He had done it before in the early morning hours of dawn.

He could not beat them all.

Liese followed, her pistol dangling at her side.

The Gestapo unit moved quietly into the lobby, past the charred remains of furniture and bones scattered in disarray. The Captain stood for a moment at the head of the staircase, smiled that strange smile of his, and descended into the basement. The troopers moved in closely behind him. The firepower was far too great. The American would not survive.

Liese did not care about the girl. All she wanted was the film and possibly the photographs, if any did exist or remain. She would hold them only for an instant, then burn them.

The Captain tried the doorknob. The door was locked.

He drew his Luger and fired once. The lock shattered.

The troopers powered their way into the basement and into a dark room of silence. The only sounds they heard were the fading chants from an old man lying on a cot. He was staring at the ceiling with eyes blinded by time and conscience. An old woman in the cot beside him had already died.

Leopold lay on the floor beside the Colonel, bullet holes neatly drilled in their heads, the work of somebody who knew how to survive when the odds had already run out on him. The soldier had crumpled against the wall. He had been clawing his throat, trying to stop the flow of blood when the second bullet ended his life. His hands still tugged at his throat.

An American was dead. There was no gun in his hand.

He was the wrong American.

Other than the old man chanting and the dead, the room was empty. Both the colonel and Leopold were naked. Theirs had not been a dignified death.

Captain Emmerich angrily whirled around to face Liese as she walked through the doorway. "You have let them escape," he screamed.

"They did not leave by the door."

"I will not tolerate failure." He shoved his Luger in her face. "Der Fuhrer does not tolerate failure," he said.

His eyes were those of a mad man, crazed and darting wildly from one side of the room to the other. Spittle was running down the side of his chin. His hand was trembling with anger.

His scream died in this throat and his eyes went blank. They lost all focus when the bullet from her Sauer 38H struck above his left eyebrow. He jerked like a puppet whose strings had been cut, and he choked on his final words.

Liese raced to the top of the stairs as he tumbled across the rigid body of the Colonel, and a spasm shot through his body for the last time. She had disappeared in the snow and was lost in the wind by the time the troopers came storming out of the clinic.

44.

AMBROSE LINCOLN DEPARTED a room where too many had already died and descended down a flight of stairs that connected the burnt-out lobby to the clinic's morgue. It had not been occupied for a long time. He had not dared escape through the front door. Somewhere out in the streets of Baden-Baden she would be waiting for him. For her, life and death was not a sudden or a rash decision. She was patient. A beautiful woman in her particular line of work had to be patient and cautious in order to survive for as long as she had. Leopold had the guile and the nerve to be an assassin. But his ego had gotten him killed. Leopold thought he was invincible.

A man who lies to himself has already condemned himself.

The words had been locked in his memory for so long that he heard the distant voice of the man who spoke them.

Harsh.

And brittle.

On the far side of the morgue, beyond the embalming table, Lincoln found a narrow metallic door, just wide enough for a gurney. A hallway stretched out before him, long and black, with a brick floor and brick walls.

Lincoln had no idea where it might lead, but he guessed that aides or interns had once wheeled the deceased – no doubt the poor, the displaced, the unwanted, the abandoned – from the morgue to their final resting place, wherever it might be.

The thought of such a walk did not disturb him.

He had spent most of his life waiting to take it.

Rachel Gruner was already wearing Leopold's woolen overcoat around her shoulders. Lincoln took the assassin's woolen hat and placed it atop her head.

"It's too big," she said.

He nodded.

"No one can see your face," he said.

Lincoln ordered the Jewish man to dress in the colonel's uniform.

The man refused.

"I will not wear the uniform of a German," he said. "I will not stoop so low." His voice was filled with defiance.

Lincoln pointed toward his wife and child. "Do you want to leave them a widow and orphan?" he asked.

"Of course not."

"Then put on the uniform." Lincoln shrugged. "The German uniform that wants to condemn you and perhaps kill you may save your life," he said.

The man wasn't pleased.

He did as he was told.

Lincoln dressed himself in Leopold's white shirt, dark woolen suit, and tie. Neither the trousers nor the coat fit him. The assassin had been far too short. But in a town tucked away in a country that had experienced the sudden discomfort and agony of war, who would take the time to notice?

He brought them all down the stairs and into the morgue.

Lincoln and the Jewish man carried the cot of the old woman who had suffered stoically and in silence during her ordeal.

"Where are you taking me?" she asked.

"We are leaving. You are leaving with us," Lincoln said.

"No," she said softly.

The old lady looked up at Lincoln and said, "Your eyes are old and have seen too much, but you still have a life to live. You all have good lives to live. Mine is ending. If the Good Lord had mercy, mine would already be over."

She paused. She glanced from face to face.

"I am staying," she said.

"I won't leave you," Lincoln said.

"You have no choice," she told him. "I have been on this earth for eighty-seven years. I lost my husband in the last war. I have been making my own decisions for a long time. Please do not dishonor me by making my last decision for me."

"You won't have a chance," Rachel said, clasping her hand.

The old lady smiled.

"But I have already had so many chances," she said. "I loved them all. Even the bad ones left me stronger."

The old lady looked up at Lincoln. "Will you need all of the guns you removed from the gentlemen upstairs?" she asked

He shook his head.

"Let me have one of the small pistols," she said. "I am old, and I am not as strong as I once was, but I can handle a small pistol. Place me on the slab before you go, and when the Germans come, and sooner or later they will come, I will stop them for as long as I can. If I have a way to provide you with a dozen more steps, then it is the way I choose to go."

"Have you ever fired a pistol before?" Lincoln asked.

She laughed.

"What's to know?"

She laughed again.

"You point and you pull the trigger," she said. She paused and looked serious for a moment. "I will be like the Old Testament. I will take my rod and smite them down."

She had a twinkle in her eye.

He grinned.

Lincoln leaned down and kissed her cheek.

He did not know why.

But he kissed her.

His mother would have been like the old lady, he thought.

His eyes saddened.

He could not remember ever having a mother.

He took the colonel's flashlight, and the rays lit up a hallway that seemed to run forever. The Jewish man and his family entered first, followed by Rachel. He took one last look into the morgue.

The lady was staring at the staircase with bitter eyes, a 9 mm Browning HP in one hand and her Torah in the other.

She glanced back at him and smiled.

He nodded and closed the heavy metallic door.

He had reached the far end of the tunnel by the time he heard the first shot. It had been the Browning HP.

45.

AGAINST ITS WILL and, no doubt, its better judgment, the Jewish section of Baden-Baden slowly began to revive itself, although it looked like a town that had been quarantined from the rest of the world. A new day had not been able to erase the tears, the sorrow, or the anger, but it was a day that none of the survivors had been promised or expected to see. For them, the past could not be salvaged or rescued, and each breath was a gift.

German soldiers – wary, perhaps a little uneasy, and heavily armed – patrolled the streets. Mostly they walked in threes, huddled closely together, their gray coats pulled tightly around their throats as they fought to protect themselves against the snow flurries and the wind.

Their faces were solemn, their eyes full of suspicion and distrust. They kept a close watch on the broken windows, the empty doorways on both sides of the street. The Jewish people were such a calm and docile people. But always there was some hot head mad enough to fight back.

He could not win, but he would take one and maybe more of them with him, before he drew his final breath. For the soldiers, it would be such an ignominious way to die. Random shots fired from the dark. It would be, they knew, a long and dangerous day.

Those on the street were stricken by a fear of the great unknown. So were those hidden on the other side of the charred walls and broken windows.

The dying had not ended.

None of them knew when it would begin again.

Ambrose Lincoln had led his party out of the morgue, down a hallway that ran, he estimated, a good seven city blocks, out a narrow doorway, and into the basement of the Synagogue.

The air around them had not been able to free itself from the pungent smell of smoke and burnt flesh.

Lincoln moved through the ruins of the sanctuary, then kept his back pressed tightly against the rock wall as he gazed out on Baden-Baden.

The street was not nearly as empty as he expected it to be. Here and there, he could see shops beginning to open up again. Older women were sweeping broken glass off the sidewalks where the snow had melted. Older men were dressed in their work clothes, and they were ambling down the street, their shovels resting on their shoulders. It was the duty of the living to throw dirt on the coffins of the dead. Life ends. And life goes on.

Their eyes were sullen. And hollow.

Their faces had lost all expression.

They had looked on the wrong side of death and knew it was only a matter of time before they, too, would lie inside a box while the living threw dirt on top of them.

As far as Ambrose Lincoln was concerned, it was now or never. He shook the Jewish man's hand, and they separated without a word, each going in different directions: a German businessman with his stylish wife, dressed in a woolen coat and matching hat, on one side of the street, and a German officer, gun barrel straight and armed with a Mauser K98 bolt action rifle, shepherding a Jewish woman and her daughter down the other.

No one bothered to look their way.

There was nothing out of the ordinary.

So many of the faces that belonged to yesterday had disappeared.

It had become a street of strangers.

Liese Himmell came into the pub from the alley and through the back door. She stood in the shadows, as motionless as a statue, and surveyed the room. Two well-dressed men sat at the bar, both

German, their beer mugs virtually empty. They were gesturing wildly, an argument over a business deal or a love gone awry, no doubt.

The bar tender was washing glasses and obviously flirting with a woman who could fall in love for five dollars and out of love when the five dollars had been spent. She was younger than she looked with straight black hair, a slit cut in the side of her short red velvet skirt, and a white blouse that had turned a faint shade of yellow by too many washings. She laughed a lot. She laughed easily. It was, Liese reasoned, her one chance to hang on to her sanity.

A lone man sat at a corner table near the front window. He was wearing wire spectacles and dressed in the straight-legged suit of a banker or maybe a funeral director, but obviously a man of means. He was smoking a cigar. He said he would be when she called him.

Liese walked quietly to the table and sat down without speaking.

He looked at her and frowned.

He blew a circle of smoke and watched it drift toward the ceiling.

"Miss Himmel, I presume," he said.

He waited for her to respond.

The code word was trolley car.

"I have not seen them today," she said.

He arched an eyebrow.

"Are the trolley cars running?" she asked.

"No," he answered. "Only the street cars."

She nodded. He was who he said he would be. On the telephone, he had called himself, Felix.

Liese smiled. He did not look like a Felix. Then again, she probably did not look like a Liese either.

"You can tell your boss that Leopold will not be bringing him the film," she said.

"It is not for certain I have a boss."

"We know Atticus quite well," she said.

"And Leopold?"

"I know him even better."

"Why do you say Leopold will not be bringing him the film?"

"Leopold is dead."

"You kill him?"

"I did not have to."

"But you would have."

"If necessary."

Felix turned away and stared out the window. "Do you have the film?" he asked without looking back at her.

"I know who does."

"Can you get it?"

"For fifty thousand U.S. dollars."

"He will not pay that much."

"It could cost him millions in lost German contracts if he refuses." She shrugged. "The American will pay a hundred thousand dollars for the film."

"Why don't you sell it to him?"

"He is not German."

"Neither is Atticus."

"But Atticus believes as we do," she said.

"And the American?"

"The American has no beliefs."

"And that makes him dangerous."

"It does."

Felix ground out the fire in his cigar and stood to leave. "Where can I find you?" he asked.

"You can't."

"So you will find me," he said.

She nodded.

"Will you have the film?"

"Will you have the fifty thousand U.S. dollars?"

"You might kill me for that much money."

Liese smiled and shrugged. "I will kill you for much less," she said and watched Felix walk wearily through the door and out into the snow.

46.

AMBROSE LINCOLN HAD always found that if he walked fast, held his head high, and seemed to be agitated and in a hurry, no one ever stopped him, not even when surrounded by enemies, and he usually was. Lincoln and Rachel crossed the street behind a German patrol.

The officer in charge scowled when he saw them but made no effort to delay or question a foreign businessman and his wife. It was obvious at a glance that he wasn't Jewish.

They forgot about him.

The patrol walked straight ahead, and Lincoln turned right. Two doors down, he escorted Rachel into the lobby of a small gasthaus. It had the two amenities he was looking for. It had locked doors, and it was open.

"Where are we going?" she asked.

"To get a room."

"Why?"

"It's a place to hide during daylight," he said. "We won't be able to go after the film until dark."

"We can't stay here," Rachel said.

"Why not?"

"I know Jacob Schneider," she said. "He owns the little gasthaus."

"We can't stay on the streets," Lincoln said flatly. "Sooner or later, someone will want to see our papers."

"We have our papers."

"But yours say you are young, strong, educated, beautiful, and Jewish." Lincoln shrugged. "That is a deadly combination to have in Baden-Baden."

"They do not say I am beautiful," she snapped.

"They should," he said.

He wasn't sure, but he thought she blushed.

Lincoln looked around the lobby. Two chairs. Blue. Worn. A newspaper draped across the arm of the nearest one. One pot plant. The plant had died. Broken glass on the floor. A mahogany writing table. Splintered. Probably an errant gunshot.

An old man behind the reception desk.

His hair was thick. And gray. He kept his pants up with frayed black suspenders.

"Is that Schneider?" he asked.

Rachel nodded. "He has known me since I was a girl."

"Can you trust him?"

"He spent many hours in our home," she said. "He and my father were like brothers. They married sisters."

Lincoln asked again, "Can you trust him."

Rachel turned away toward the door.

"No," she said.

"Why not?"

"His hotel is open," she answered. "The others on the street still lie in rubble. It may be a coincidence. It may not."

"Perhaps he was lucky."

"Maybe."

"But you doubt it."

"When I was a small girl and my mama was still alive, my father showed Mr. Schneider a wool coat he wanted to buy." Rachel folded her arms and walked to the front window, which was little more than splintered glass. "Winter was coming. My father's coat was threadbare," she said. "He had been saving for two years to buy the coat. It was made from pure wool and thick enough to protect him from the cold and the rains. He went back to buy the coat, and it was gone."

"Schneider?"

"When we saw him next, he was wearing the coat." Rachel shook her head. "My father forgave him. I did not."

Lincoln took her arm, and they walked to the reception desk together.

"One room," he said.

Jacob's eyes passed Lincoln and focused on Rachel. His face turned a faint shade of pale.

"I thought you were dead," he said.

"It was not my night to die," Rachel said. She forced a thin smile.

"So many of us did." Schneider lowered his eyes.

"But not you," Rachel said.

"No," said Schneider, "not me. I was in Strasbourg when the attack came. Business. I was buying new furniture. As you see, my chairs are quite old and frayed."

"How convenient," Rachel said.

Schneider stared at her without speaking.

Lincoln watched his eyes, always, the eyes. The pupils were darker now and dilated. Lincoln knew that, given a reason and perhaps a pocketful of spare change, Schneider would betray them.

He placed forty marks on the desk.

"This for the room," he said.

Lincoln placed a single bullet beside the bills.

"This is for you," he said.

Schneider's chin quivered. "I don't understand," he said, and his voice cracked.

"We do not want to be disturbed," Lincoln said.

"Your passport?"

"I will keep my passport."

"But the law says I must retain your passport for my files as long as you are my guest at the hotel." Schneider's words were tumbling over each other.

Lincoln picked up the bullet and dropped it in his coat pocket. "The law no longer applies," he said.

"What if the Germans ask for it?"

"Your answer to them is quite simple," Lincoln said.

"What's that?"

"We were never here." Lincoln's smile was as cold as his eyes. "I would like the key, please," he said.

"Which room?"

"To the room that has not been rented to anyone."

"First floor?"

"I prefer the third."

Schneider handed him the key to room three twenty-six.

"You will not be here when we leave," Lincoln said.

"No."

"It's better that way."

He and Rachel walked briskly up the staircase to the third floor. On the landing, Lincoln dropped the key in a trash can littered with newspapers and stale cigarette butts.

"What are you doing?" Rachel asked.

"We are staying in a different room."

"We don't have a key."

Lincoln shrugged and grinned. "But Schneider won't have our room number," he said. "If the Germans come, he will sell us out cheaply. They will go to the wrong room, and we will hear them, which buys us an extra two minutes to be gone before they find us."

Rachel frowned. "You have done this before," she said.

"I guess," Lincoln answered. "It does feel familiar."

"You are a strange man," Rachel said.

"You're not the first to figure that out about me," he said.

He selected room three forty-four with a window beside the fire escape, picked the lock and walked in. Small room. Small bed. It would work just fine, he thought.

"We'll get some rest and be ready to leave just after dusk," Lincoln said.

"Will I have time for a shower?" Rachel asked.

"I don't see why not."

A look of fear crossed her face. "But what if the Germans come while I am bathing?" she asked.

Lincoln removed his coat and slumped in the chair facing the door. He closed his eyes and remembered the words of the little old lady who had chosen to stay and fight her last battle in the morgue.

"Don't worry," he said.

"Why not?"

"I will smite them down," he said.

47.

AMBROSE LINCOLN SAT with his eyes on the window, watching as the day wore on into the afternoon. The snow came in spurts, sometimes a blizzard, sometimes little more than scattered flakes tossed around by the winds. A strange silence had fallen over the Jewish sector of Baden-Baden. There were dead to mourn, dead to bury, and no one to grieve at a Synagogue that, after the fire, deserved its own eulogy.

German soldiers moved down the streets, keeping their backs to the wind. An occasional jeep crept from one alley to another. A Jewish boy not more than sixteen was being dragged along the sidewalk by two members of the Gestapo guard. His safe house was no longer a hiding place, and Lincoln saw a column of black smoke rising above a little shop.

A man and his wife stood in the doorway.

He was wringing his hands.

She was crying.

All they had were gone.

The shop.

And the son.

They might rebuild the shop.

The son would not be coming home.

Rachel walked out of the steam that had gathered in the bathroom. Her hair was wet around her face. She had wrapped a towel around her. Droplets of hot water were clustered on her neck and shoulders.

"I washed the dress," she explained. "It won't take long to dry."

Lincoln nodded.

He watched her sit down on the bed. She was a blending of beauty and sadness, no different from the old couple on the street.

All she had was gone.

A home.

A job.

A classroom.

A father.

But she had the film.

And so many had already died trying to possess it.

The possibility of war hung in the balance.

He turned his attention back to streets below. They told him little. In time, he guessed, they would tell him all.

"Where will you go when this is over?" he said.

"I don't know."

"You can't stay here," he said.

"Nobody wants to harm me," she said. "They simply want the film. When I no longer have it, they will no longer care about me."

"If you give the film to me," Lincoln said, "they will kill you."

"Why?"

"They will feel you have betrayed them."

"I am only doing what my father wanted," she said.

"They feel your father betrayed them."

"He died because he wanted the world to know."

"What?"

"That Germany is lying." She sighed and leaned back on the bedpost. "I have read the newspapers," she said. "I know the lies being told. Germany says it does not want to harm the Jews. Germany says that we will be able to live as free people. But Germany wants to eliminate us all."

"I've never understood why."

"Germany is jealous of us," she said.

"It's that simple?"

Rachel laughed softly. "Jews have done well in business," she said. "Germany has the men and the power and a war machine, but we have the money. Germany wants to take it. If we are gone, Germany will never have to give it back."

"That's why you must leave here," Lincoln said.

"But I have no money," she said.

"It doesn't matter."

"Why should I leave when my people are here?"

"Who is here to protect you?"

"I can take care of myself."

"You will be running for the rest of your life," Lincoln said. "You won't sleep at night. You will fear the shadows because you don't know who is hiding in them. Friends will turn on friends. The ones you trust most will sell you to the Germans, and they will die before they ever spend the blood money."

Rachel closed her eyes and shivered. She pulled the quilt tighter around her. "I have no choice," she said.

"You have a choice," Lincoln said.

"What are you suggesting?"

"You can leave with me."

"And where are you going?"

"Away."

"And what would you want with me."

Lincoln was still staring out the window.

But he smiled.

And she saw the smile.

And it was the only thing gentle about him she had ever seen. Rachel stood and walked across the room and kissed him lightly on the cheek.

No words were spoken.

Lincoln placed his arm around her, and Rachel sat on the padded arm of the chair.

In silence, they watched the street below.

"Is that your job?" Rachel finally asked.

"What's that?"

"You kill people."

"No," he said, "I fix things."

"Can you fix me?" she asked.

He watched the snow grow heavy outside the window.

"I can try," he said.

48.

THE GERMANS DIDN'T come until late in the day when the last remnants of daylight were scurrying back toward the darkness. Ambrose Lincoln heard their footsteps on the staircase. Not even the padding in the carpet could deaden the sounds.

What a man hears can keep him alive longer than what he sees.

He heard the words echo from somewhere in deep recesses of his mind.

Harsh.

And brittle.

He sighed wearily. Perhaps the old man down at the reception desk had called them. Perhaps there was a reward. Perhaps he was only trying to save his own skin. Perhaps he was trying to make sure none of them burned his gasthaus. Perhaps the Gestapo guard was merely going from building to building throughout the Jewish sector, searching every possible nook and cranny where he and the girl, especially the girl, might be hiding.

Lincoln stood and walked across the room.

Rachel Gruner lay sleeping on top of the bed. She had gone to sleep with her hair still wet, and it appeared frazzled and curly on the ends.

He gently shook her shoulders.

Her eyes opened with a start.

"It's time to go," he whispered.

By now, she could hear the footsteps on the stairs as well. At least one soldier and maybe more had begun walking down the hallway. One was trying to unlock the door, probably three-twenty-six.

The guard would not find them there.

Lincoln had bought two minutes, maybe five.

It was enough.

He traveled light.

Rachel swung her legs off the bed and reached for the woolen coat. She put it on as she walked toward the far side of the room. Lincoln placed the woolen hat on her head and raised the window.

The cold wind had a bite.

The snow was falling harder now.

The streets of Baden-Baden were barely visible in the dying minutes of dusk.

Lincoln climbed out onto the fire escape, then took her hand and helped Rachel through the window. She shivered. Maybe from the cold. Maybe not.

With his arm wrapped around her, they worked their way slowly down the three flights. Ice had formed a thick sheet on the rungs, and each step was a bold and precarious expression of faith. A fall. A broken bone. It would be the end for them. The cold, the exposure to the snow and wind, could be as deadly as a German Luger. The early night grew darker.

Lincoln removed the Heckler and Koch semi-automatic pistol from his belt. His eyes swept down the street. Almost all signs of life had vanished into a shelter. A stray dog rummaged among the trash cans. A patrol jeep eased slowly around the far corner, its headlights blurred by the falling snow. The jeep moved on past, and Lincoln waited until the red tail lights dimmed and finally vanished. A few shops had lights burning in an upstairs window.

He dropped the eight feet to the sidewalk.

Rachel followed.

He caught her and broke her fall. She winced as an ankle bent awkwardly beneath her. She knelt in the snow and tried to rub the pain away.

"You all right?" he whispered.

She nodded.

Lincoln heard muffled voices above them.

He pulled Rachel back against the brick wall of the gasthaus and looked up through the skeletal rungs and railings of the fire escape.

One German soldier was looking out the window.

He was talking frantically. No doubt cursing his misfortune, Lincoln told himself. The wind was blowing the words away. The snowfall had grown more intense.

It was a perfect night, Lincoln thought. No one was foolish enough to be out on a night like this. That's what the Germans would think. Only a madman would risk it. Ambrose Lincoln was a madman. He knew the darkness and the snow would hide them.

"Where is the film?" he asked Rachel.

"Not far."

He looked up again.

The German had gone.

They had six more rooms to search.

That gave him a ten-minute head start.

Lincoln smiled. He had started and ended a war in less time.

He looked down at Rachel. "Which way?" he asked.

"Follow me," she said.

They walked arm-in-arm gingerly down the sidewalk of a town without pity, compassion, or remorse. The snow had long buried the splinters of broken glass. Fires had burned themselves out. Those who had been herded away would not be coming back. Those left behind would learn to survive without them. They shared a grief and a loneliness they would take to their graves. The young would endure, Lincoln knew. The young always did. They would not learn from their mistakes, but they would persist and survive. The old felt cheated. Death had left them in misery. Death could have been so kind to them.

But death was unfair.

Death passed them by.

Rachel led them through a terraced garden behind her father's photographic studio and turned down a narrow, cobblestone alleyway that led toward the back of the synagogue. Her face was numb. She had to squint hard to look past the cluster of flakes collecting on her eyelashes.

"It's not far," she said.

They waited in the shadows while the jeep rolled past. The German soldiers were huddled inside, trying without much luck to keep out the cold. They may have been on patrol. They were no longer searching for anyone.

Anybody out on a night like this would not be alive come morning.

"Where have you hidden the film?" Lincoln asked.

"My father has it," she said.

"I thought your father was dead."

"He is," she said.

She ran across the street and was stopped by a wrought iron gate whose latch had been frozen in place. Lincoln used the butt of his pistol to chip the ice away. On the far side of the fence, he saw only the faint outlines of stone grave markers.

49.

THE SNOW CRUNCHED beneath their feet as they moved cautiously through the tombstones. Ambrose Lincoln glanced at each marker as he passed. Lives, both long and short, had been reduced to a handful of words and numbers. Only two dates were apparently important in a person's existence. The day of birth. And the day of Death. Everything in between was only a memory. The wind howled at his ears, and only a few flakes were falling among the trees. A half moon had broken through the clouds, and a pale shaft of light was touching the ground around them.

Lincoln would have preferred the darkness.

The hand holding his Heckler and Koch semi-automatic had grown numb and lost all feeling.

Rachel led him past the markers and on toward the backside of the cemetery where a simple plot of empty land was covered by several rows of recently dug graves, now buried in the snow.

Lincoln counted twenty-seven of them.

He saw only the mounds of raw dirt.

No stones.

No names.

He and Rachel were not alone.

Lincoln saw her standing alone beside a grave that had been detached from the others. It was larger. He figured it was the first.

His eyes fell on the small, oval face of a young woman, maybe thirty, maybe not, with long raven hair and a beauty mark or a spot of mud under her left eye. She was barely five feet tall and wore a woolen dress the color of the earth. Her skin was pale, translucent, and had not yet been touched by the sun. She was barefoot in the snow and carrying a bleached cotton sack. Her eyes were dark, filled with bitterness and regret.

She looked at him and smiled.

"Is your child with you?" he asked.

She nodded.

And a tear removed the smile.

You will not let them forget, she said.

"No."

You must not let them forget.

"I won't," he whispered.

They have lied, she said.

"I know," he said.

He watched her move in a ghostly silence back through the cemetery, her bare feet walking on top of the snow as though she had not touched it at all, a small girl by her side. They were holding hands when they disappeared into the mist.

Rachel was staring at him with a strange expression on her face.

"What's wrong?" she asked.

He shook his head and looked away.

"Who were you talking to?" she asked.

"I talk a lot in cemeteries," he said.

"Does anyone ever talk back?" she asked.

"Sometimes," he said.

She continued staring at him, frowning, trying to understand a man who was so gentle, so tender, so loving, and yet could kill so easily, wondering who or what had shattered him and if anyone would ever be able to put the scattered pieces of his mind back together again.

Rachel waited for him go on.

He didn't.

His focus had shifted elsewhere, back to the graves, the final home for those who had lost their homes and had nowhere else to go.

Rachel let her gaze sweep across the unmarked mounds.

"It's so different," she said.

Lincoln remained silent.

"There were only three graves that first night," she said. "Now there are so many." She choked back a sob. "I don't know where my father is buried."

"And he has the film."

"I did not know where to hide the film," she said. "Everything was burning. Everything was in ruin. Nothing was safe or sacred, and I did not know what to do. I brought the film here and left it with him. They would not search among the dead."

Lincoln wrapped an arm around her. He could feel her shivering and not from the cold. He held her against his chest until the trembling stopped.

"Take your time," he said. "Close your eyes. Concentrate on that night. In your mind, do your best to recreate that night. Remember everything you saw. Where were the first two graves? Was your father's grave to the left of them, or to the right?"

The silence was broken by a voice.

"She will not find her father's grave," it said.

Ambrose Lincoln wheeled around with his Heckler and Koch pistol at eye level. Where had the man been hiding, he wondered. Why hadn't he seen him? Why had he allowed himself to be distracted?

Men may survive one mistake. He had heard the voice before. They seldom survive the second one. The unexpected brings with it the final bullet.

The voice was harsh.

And brittle.

Ambrose Lincoln was staring into the face of an aging Jewish man. He was short, rotund, had lost most of his gray hair, and had seen far too much in too short a time. He did not appear to be frightened by the gun. He was looking at Rachel. As far as he was concerned, Lincoln was not with them in the cemetery.

Rachel ran to the old man and hugged him: Samuel Feichtmann. The baker down the street. She had eaten black bread from his shop almost every day of her life. He was her last link with the near and recent past.

He squeezed her tightly.

She did not want him to let her go.

"Where is my father's grave?" she whispered.

"The Germans came for him."

"The Germans had already killed him."

"The Gestapo thought he might have been buried with his camera." The old man shrugged. "They thought they might find the film with the camera. Someone had given them a map of each grave and who was buried in it."

"He was buried with the film," Rachel said.

"I know," the old man said.

"Did they find the film?" Rachel asked with a quiver in her voice. "No."

"Did they take my father?"

"No," Feichtmann said.

"They took poor old Mister Mendelssohn. I did not trust the Germans, so I switched their graves."

"Where is my father now?"

"Second row, third grave from the left," Feichtmann said. He turned to Lincoln and handed him the shovel. "I am too old for this," he said.

Lincoln nodded and walked to the second row of graves, counted three to the left, and began to dig. The blade of his shovel struck the box under a foot of snow and only six inches of dirt.

He pried the lid open.

Benjamin Gruner looked as though he were only sleeping, preserved by the cold. The blood had been washed from his face. Lincoln forced the old man's rigid hands open and found five rolls of film. He removed them, dropped the rolls in his pocket, and quickly hammered the lid back in place.

He threw dirt and snow on top of the coffin, and by morning, if the snow kept falling, no one would ever know that Benjamin Gruner had been visited in the night. He glanced around and saw Rachel walking toward the gate, a single shadow among many. Feichtmann was nowhere in sight. The clouds had reclaimed the moon, and he was left in a cemetery as dark as the inside of the caskets lying beneath the snow.

Lincoln leaned the shovel against the trunk of a crooked old oak.

The shovel had not dug its final grave.

50.

THE WIND CAME blowing hard across the Potomac, and the big man sitting alone on a park bench glanced up at the thick gray clouds hanging low and uneasy over the city. The weatherman had promised a light snow before night, and he could already feel an icy mist in the air. Atticus Chandler leaned forward, bracing himself against his cane, and watched the German industrialist walk slowly up the flat stone walkway. Atticus looked up at the clock on the side of the government building and smiled. It was four-thirty, give or take a couple of minutes. Rudolph Hinkel was right on time.

Then again, he should be.

Rudolph Hinkel had called the meeting.

"We have a problem," he said.

Atticus shrugged. "We always have a problem," Atticus replied. "It's the nature of our business. My only concern is why we aren't discussing the problem in a nice warm gentleman's club, maybe in front of a roaring fireplace, with a bottle of Benedictine and Brandy between us."

"I thought you would prefer privacy."

"I prefer warm."

"No one can hear us out here," Rudolph said.

"No one else is stupid enough to be out here on a day like this."

Rudolph gazed across the Potomac.

Atticus waited.

He wished he had worn gloves.

"Leopold is dead," Rudolph said.

"When?" Atticus was working hard to hide his emotions.

"We don't know."

"How?"

"He was shot."

Atticus slammed his cane against the pavement in a sudden outburst of anger. "The American?" he asked.

"From what I have been told, Leopold had him trapped," Rudolph said. "One way in. No other way out."

"So he walked into the middle of his own trap."

"Apparently so."

Atticus spit in disgust. The spittle turned to ice as soon as it touched the ground. "And the girl?"

"She was with the American."

"So he had found her."

"Apparently so," Rudolph repeated.

"And Leopold could not."

"Leopold found both of them," Rudolph said. "As I understand it, his orders were to eliminate them as quickly as possible."

Atticus scowled. "His orders were to find the film and destroy it," he said.

"He made a mistake."

"Damn costly mistake."

"Apparently so."

"So the girl or the American or both of them still have the film," Atticus said.

"We are not sure that the film even exists," Rudolph replied.

"Are you willing to take that chance?" Atticus asked. He stood and began walking toward the river even though the wind was blowing cold in his face. The square-faced German industrialist followed, as Atticus knew he would. "Are you and Germany both willing to lose twenty million dollars worth of government contracts, which will surely happen, if the film does exist, and the photographs suddenly show up on the President's desk and the front page of every newspaper in this country? It could ruin us."

"We may have a solution," Rudolph said.

"It had better be a damn good one."

"I received a phone call early this morning."

"Just before you called me to arrange our meeting?"

"Yes."

"It must have been damned important."

"It was."

"Go on."

Atticus returned to the bench and seated himself, pulling his heavy coat tighter around his face. Rudolph sat down beside him, staring straight across the river. The wind had reddened his face, and a light snow had begun to fall on his thick, gray hair.

"There are those in German business and the Third Reich who are as worried as you are about the photographs being released," Rudolph said.

Atticus nodded.

"They hired their own operative to find the girl and take the film." Rudolph paused a moment, then continued, "The operative was working for an officer with the Gestapo. He was apparently killed in the same firefight that cost you Leopold. The operative no longer has a contact within the German government and has, so to speak, been left out in the cold."

"And has called you."

"Yes."

"To make a deal."

"The operative wants fifty thousand dollars," Rudolph said.

Atticus felt his hand grow tighter on the handle of his cane. He was a man who dictated the terms of any deal. He did not like them being dictated to him. "That's a lot of money," he said.

"That's up front," Rudolph said. "The operative wants another fifty thousand dollars when the film is delivered to you."

"That's robbery."

Rudolph shrugged and chuckled. "That's business," he said. "What will it cost you if the photographs make their way to the President's desk, which gives him the proof he needs to go to war with Germany?"

"Millions." Atticus slumped over his cane. "I would hate to estimate the number of millions it would cost me and you both," he said.

"What the operative wants is pocket change," Rudolph said.

"Can the operative deliver?"

"She says she can."

Atticus jerked his head around. The scowl returned to his face. "Did you say *she*?" he asked.

Rudolph nodded.

"We are putting our fate in the hands of a woman?"

The blood was draining from Atticus Chandler's face.

Rudolph nodded again.

"That's ludicrous," Atticus said.

"Look at it another way," Rudolph said.

"What other way?"

"Leopold and the Gestapo officer are dead," Rudolph said. "She isn't."

"She may have killed them both to make the deal for herself," Atticus spit out. "She may have gotten greedy and decided to work for both sides."

"If she gets us the film, does it really matter?"

Atticus thought it over for a minute.

"No," he said. "Where am I supposed to send the money?"

Rudolph handed him a piece of paper with the proper banking information written in ink.

"She wants Marks," he said.

"She obviously thinks Germany will win any war in Europe."

Rudolph smiled. "Don't we all?" he asked.

The snow was falling harder now, and by the time Rudolph reached the far edge of the park, his footprints had been erased as though he had never been to a meeting with Atticus at all.

51.

SHE WALKED DOWN the hallway of the German Embassy as though she owned the place. Hers was not an unrecognized face. Tall. Blonde. Mostly legs, although it was difficult to tell beneath the long, black leather coat with a hemline that almost reached the floor. She had the collar pulled up around her neck.

Liese Himmel looked neither left nor right, but straight ahead at the office of Colonel Hartman, the commandant of the Gestapo guards in Baden-Baden, waiting at the end of the narrow hall. She had been offered an escort but refused, and no one pressed the issue.

She opened the door and walked in. An aide at the reception desk stood to stop her. She ignored him and burst into the colonel's office.

Hartman looked up from the map taped atop his desk. He had been drawing lines connecting cities, airports, and railroad terminals.

"Do you have an appointment?" he asked.

"It's not necessary for me to have one," she answered.

"In my office, it is."

"Then we must move your office," she said.

Hartman glared at her.

"I can have you removed," the colonel said

"But you won't."

The colonel studied her for a moment, then shrugged with resignation. "I'm sure there is a reason for you to disturb me as you have," he said.

He motioned Liese to have a seat across the desk from him.

She remained standing. "I have come to make sure that our business arrangement is still in place," she said.

Hartman grinned savagely. All of the humor had vanished from his eyes long ago. He was lean and wiry, not yet fifty, a man who had spent most of his life either fighting wars or planning them.

"I understand you worked for Captain Emmerich," he said.

"Captain Emmerich drew up the arrangement."

The colonel leaned back in his chair and cocked his head to the right. "I'm afraid that the captain is no longer employed here."

"I know," Liese said. "I was there."

"Then you know that any business arrangement signed by Captain Emmerich is no longer valid."

"He was representing Germany," she said calmly. "He was representing the Third Reich. He was representing the Gestapo."

Hartman laughed out loud.

"No," he said, "Captain Emmerich was only representing himself."

"He believed the film was important to the cause."

Hartman shrugged. "It may have been important to his cause," Hartman said. "But not to mine. Personally, I doubt if any such film exists. Besides, what can it reveal about that night? A few drunken students started protesting. It got out of hand and caused a little trouble. Nothing serious. That's all. "

"People died."

Hartman shrugged. "People die every day."

"Women and children were murdered."

"That's what happens in war." Hartman's grin grew broader, and he clasped his hands together under his chin.

Liese leaned forward and placed both hands on top of the desk. "We are not at war."

Hartman laughed again. Harder this time. "We have always been at war," he said. Colonel Hartman stood and walked around the desk. His eyes narrowed.

A sense of hidden anger began to rise up within him. "As long as an inferior race of people denigrate and desecrate our homeland, we will be at war until they have been removed from Germany and eliminated from the face of the earth."

"You have thus far been able to do it quietly."

"We have indeed."

"If the images on the film show what a lot of people think they do," Liese said, "then the whole world will know of your secret little war against the Jews, and they will stop you."

"They will do nothing."

"You may underestimate them."

"No," the colonel said. "Their politicians will make speeches. They will get angry for a while. Their governments will even threaten us. But in the end, they will watch what we do, complain about what we do, and do nothing."

He walked to the doorway into his office and asked, "Who is working the kitchen this afternoon?"

His aide glanced of the daily worksheet and said, "Bergner."

"Can he climb?"

"He can."

"Take him to the tree."

The aide walked out of the office. Colonel Hartman moved behind his desk, and raised the window. He stood in the face of a harsh wind that was blowing snow in from off the streets.

Liese glanced out the window and watched an old man in striped pajamas being dragged across the yard behind the embassy. He was barefoot. His glasses had been broken. He was trembling in the cold.

Bergner – she assumed it was Bergner – was thrown to the bottom of a tree growing just outside the window.

She heard the German guards cursing him, but the words they spoke were scattered by the winds.

The old man grabbed the trunk of the tree and straightened himself. He looked up, into a white, heavy laden sky, bowed his head in a silent prayer, and began to climb, one limb at a time. His ascent was slow and arduous. Once, he almost fell. He kept climbing. Slowly and methodically. But he was climbing.

Hartman had run out of patience.

As Bergman reached the fifth limb, the colonel leaned out the window and yelled to the Jew, "Flap your wings like a bird."

He did.

He was frightened. He would do whatever they wanted.

He kept flapping, waiting for someone to tell him to stop.

Hartman pulled a Luger from its holster and shot the man once in the head.

The Jew tumbled through the trees and into the snow. He had died without ever seeing death coming his way.

Hartman whirled around, gun in hand, and stared at Liese. "The world may try to condemn us," he said, "but the world will never be able to convict us of shooting birds from our trees."

He glanced back out the window. The guards were dragging Bergman away, and traces of blood stained the snow.

When he turned again to Liese, she had her Browning HP inches away from his forehead.

He raised his eyebrows in surprise.

She put a bullet between both of them, turned, and walked briskly down the hallway.

In the foyer, a Gestapo guard stopped her. "Was Hartman hunting for birds again?"

"He was."

The guard laughed. "I thought I heard two shots," he said.

"Target practice," Liese said and walked out of the embassy and into a day growing dark, but not as dark as the inside of a dead man's soul.

52.

AMBROSE LINCOLN COULD see the German sentry waving for him and Rachel to stop before they reached the intersection. He felt Rachel's hand growing tighter on his arm. The snow was falling heavily, and the flakes were large and wet. A harsh and ragged wind cut sharply down the streets.

"Keep your head up," he whispered loudly.

"They will recognize me."

"They are strangers in your midst," he said calmly. "You are equally a stranger in theirs. If you lower your head, they feel you have something to hide. The secret is to be respectful but as arrogant as they are."

Lincoln stopped as the sentry approached him, removed his papers from his coat pocket, and handed them to the sentry.

The German was young.

He was cold.

He was not cut out for killing.

He was only doing what he had been ordered to do.

The sentry scanned the papers and handed them back. "It's a cold day to be on the streets, Mister Wagner," he said.

"Duty calls, I'm afraid."

"Your documents say you are a professor."

"I am."

"There is no school open anywhere in Baden-Baden today."

Lincoln shrugged and stuck the papers in his pocket. "I have a lecture this afternoon on campus," he said.

"The subject of your lecture?"

"The growing concern about the world financial system," he said

The sentry frowned.

"Is there a problem with the system?" he asked.

Lincoln smiled. "Not if you live in Germany," he said.

The sentry grinned broadly. He nodded toward Rachel.

"Do you have the papers for the lady?" he asked.

"She is my wife."

"She must have papers."

Lincoln smiled apologetically. "I am afraid they are back in the room," he said. "In our haste, we neglected to pick them up. We will be happy to go get them if we must."

"It's imperative." The sentry paused and wiped the snow from his collar. "I regret it for your sake," he said. "But no one is allowed on the street without proper credentials. I would let you pass if I were in charge, Herr Wagner. Unfortunately, I am not. They are watching me from across the street."

"It was our error, not yours," he said.

"I hope this will not delay your lecture, sir," he said.

"We have plenty of time."

Ambrose Lincoln and Rachel turned around and walked back up the sidewalk, their boots scraping shards of shattered glass in the snow.

"He was expecting us," Rachel said softly.

"It was not a coincidence," Lincoln said.

The sentry watched them walk away, then turned and nodded to a lone figure standing across the street.

Tall.

Blonde.

Wrapped in a black leather coat.

Liese Himmel nodded back.

The sentry fingered the fresh roll of fifty marks in his pocket. It was a cold, worthless day on the streets, perhaps, but not unprofitable.

His job was done, and the woman had paid him well. He stepped inside a small pub and soaked up the warmth from a wood burning stove beside the bar. He glanced at the clock on the wall. It was two-thirty, definitely not too early for a beer. He was the only one in the room.

The pub owner had vanished on the Night of Broken Glass.

He would not be coming back.

Soldiers kept the pub open.

Plenty of beer.

Free beer.

They stoked the stove with the scrap lumber from homes that had been torn down and destroyed.

The fire chased away the cold for a while, and the soldiers kept reminding each other that the supply of beer in the warehouse behind the bar was sufficient enough to keep them supplied with strong drink until the war was over, provided there was a war and it didn't last too long.

Ambrose Lincoln and Rachel walked two blocks into the driving snow until he was convinced that they were no longer visible to the German sentry. The falling snow had erased their trail. He cut sharply into an alley and stood with his back pressed against the brick wall, out of the wind. Snow continued to pile up at his feet.

A faint aroma of food drifted down the alley.

It had been two days since he had eaten, maybe more for Rachel. He didn't know. She had not complained.

"A café?" he asked her.

"There was," Rachel said softly. "I don't know if there is."

"Somebody's cooking."

"Before the night when the Germans came," she said, "my father and I ate at the little café around the corner twice a week, sometimes more."

"No reason to leave the city on an empty stomach," Lincoln said.

"Or die on one," she said.

They walked a block down the alley and crossed the street.

On the corner, they saw a small sign in the window that said: *Weingarten Café.*

A light was shining inside.

The tables were set, a bottle of wine placed atop each one.

The dining room was empty.

Lincoln and Rachel were met inside by a matronly little woman, shaped like a dumpling with gray hair. Her face was ashen. She saw Rachel and began to tremble.

"You cannot stay here," she said.

"We only want a lunch," Lincoln said. "We can pay."

She ignored him but grabbed Rachel by both arms. "They are looking for you," she said.

"Who?"

"Everyone." She nervously rubbed her hands together. "I hear them talk. Powerful people in the Reich want you dead. If they find you with me, they will want me dead, too."

"Are they watching?"

"They are always watching."

"Do the Germans ever come to the kitchen?" Lincoln asked.

The woman shook her head.

"We can eat in the kitchen," he said.

"You must eat and leave quickly."

"Thank you, Mrs. Bergner," Rachel said.

"They have come for all of us," the old woman said as she walked out of the dining room. "My husband was taken on the first night."

"Where was he taken?" Lincoln asked.

"No one knows," the old woman said. "The men, mostly the young men, are simply marched away and dropped off the far side of the earth."

Rachel patted her shoulder to comfort her. "I'm sure Mister Bergner will be back soon," she said.

"No," the old woman said. "He will not be coming back." She shrugged. "I will be going to meet him."

She smiled.

"I don't think it will be long," she said.

53.

THE STEW WAS a godsend. Mostly vegetables. Little meat. Cooked to perfection. It may have just been he was hungry. The old woman had merely brought them two bowls, still steaming, and left them alone. Lincoln was able to hear voices in the dining room, interrupted by an occasional laugh. German soldiers coming in for dinner, he guessed.

The language they used was far too coarse and crude to be mistaken for the poetry of nobility. He left ten marks beneath a pitcher on the counter, took Rachel's arm, and escorted her through the back door and out into the alley.

Lincoln looked both ways.

Nothing.

And that troubled him a great deal.

Baden-Baden was no different from the remote woodlands. When the predator was stalking his prey, the forest grew quiet.

Nothing moved.

There were no sounds.

Even the birds quit singing.

It was a quiet prelude to death.

He listened.

Nothing.

Only silence.

It was deafening.

"Should we wait for dark?" Rachel asked.

"We should." Lincoln held her tightly against him. "We don't have time," he said.

"Then we shall go now."

"Keep your head up."

"What if the sentries stop us again?"

"They won't."

"Why not?"

"We know they are out there this time," Lincoln said.

"You will shoot them," Rachel said.

"If necessary."

Rachel walked in silence for a block, then asked, "Does it ever bother you?" she asked.

"What?"

"Killing so many people," Rachel said.

"I don't plan to kill them," Lincoln said without expression. "But when they shove a gun in my face and ask to die, I feel as though it's my duty to oblige."

"Do you ever have nightmares?"

"Seldom."

"I would close my eyes and see the faces of the dead," Rachel said.

"It's better than closing your eyes and never waking up," he said.

"I wonder."

Lincoln smiled. "I wonder, too, sometimes," he said.

Rachel led him into the burnt-out building that had served as her home and her father's photographic studio.

"Can you develop the film?" Lincoln asked.

"If the chemicals have not been spilled."

"And make some prints."

"How many?" she asked.

"Enough to make sure that the world sees what your father wanted it to see," Lincoln said. "We have five rolls of film. That's all. If we lose any of them, if any of them are taken from us, they are lost and gone forever. I would like to have several sets of prints. Then if we lose the film, the pictures will still exist. I can mail them to three different addresses I have: one in Washington, D. C., one in

New York, and one in Amsterdam. We may lose some of them. We won't lose them all."

"Who wants the film so badly to send you after it?" Rachel asked.

"I don't know."

"Have you ever known?"

"No."

"Aren't you ever curious?"

"No."

"You just do it for the money, I guess."

"I do it because I am asked to do it," Lincoln said.

Rachel walked into the darkroom and looked around. It lay in disarray. Her father had always been so neat, so organized, so orderly. He would be appalled to see the mess she had discovered.

Trays had been bent, stomped on, and left scattered on the floor. The room reeked of the odor of strong chemicals spilled on the floor and left to dry. The enlarger had been broken in half, and its skeletal remains lay in the sink.

The water had been turned off.

Print paper, so sensitive to light, had been taken from their boxes and thrown about the room. Any light that might have worked its way through the cracks in the walls and broken windows would have already ruined the sheets by now.

They had the film.

There would be no prints.

Not in Baden-Baden anyway.

"How long did your father have his business?" Lincoln asked.

"It would have been thirty three years next March," Rachel said.

"A lifetime in the making," Lincoln said, "and destroyed in minutes."

Rachel walked out the door. "I'm going to see if there any clothes I can salvage from my room," she said.

"How long will you be in there?"

"Ten minutes at the most."

"I'll wait for you."

She was gone.

Her shadow was nowhere to be seen, but he saw the others playing upon the wall, always the shadows, always condemning him. Ambrose Lincoln had never been able to escape the shadows. Most of them he remembered. He did not trust the new ones.

After ten minutes, he closed her father's cabinet one last time and went to look for her.

Lincoln saw Rachel at the top of the stairs.

She had changed dresses.

It was dark and somber.

Her eyes were wide with fright.

The cold metal barrel of a Browning HP was jammed against her right temple.

Liese Himmel's finger was on the trigger.

Liese was smiling.

"The film, please," she said. "I don't want to hurt her or kill you. But I will do what is necessary to acquire the film. I would try to buy it, but I know you won't sell it, so I will trade her life for the five rolls of film."

The wind slammed a shutter against the window.

Rachel caught her breath.

It sounded like a pistol shot.

54.

THE Browning HP NEVER wavered. Rachel had tried to scream, but her throat was tightened with fear. Her legs went limp, and she slid to the floor. Liese grabbed her hair and held the girl upright, pressing the barrel of the Browning HP against the top of her head. Rachel was staring at Ambrose Lincoln with terrified eyes that held no sign of hope. Liese kept staring at Ambrose Lincoln with cold, steady eyes that held no signs of either doubt or remorse.

Lincoln had seen those kinds of eyes before.

He saw them every morning when he looked into the mirror.

They were eyes that – because of time, distance, and circumstance – had been separated from the soul of mankind.

"I am tired of chasing you," Liese said.

"I'm tired of running."

"It ends here," Liese said.

"No," Lincoln said. "Nothing ends here. Rachel may die. I may die. Or we all may die. But those who hate will continue to hate and those who fight will continue to fight. When it's all over and the ground is full of graves, people will pass by our bones, and they won't care who died or when we died, or why we died, or if we had ever walked the streets of Baden-Baden. And the fighting goes on. Nothing ends, Liese."

"For us, it will."

"It doesn't have to," Lincoln said.

"No, it doesn't."

Rachel's shoulders had grown rigid. Her face was pale, her head bowed, her eyes closed. There was nothing for her to do but brace herself and wait for the bullet that would surely come.

"The film is of no importance to you," Liese said.

"It's important to those I work for."

"Whose side are they on?"

"I don't know."

"And you, Mister Lincoln, whose side are you on."

"The ones who died here."

"Did you know them?"

"No."

"Did you ever meet them?"

"No."

"Then they don't matter anymore," Liese said. "All that matters are three lives. Mine. Yours. And the girl's. Forget about the Jews. Forget about the Germans, Forget about the rich and powerful who deposit money in your bank. Forget about the madman in Berlin. For them, life goes on. It may be good or bad. I don't know. But life goes on. I'd just as soon see life go on for us as well."

"So you just expect me to give you the film," Lincoln said.

"I do."

"Without a fight."

"It's better that way." Liese smiled sadly. "Here is the situation," she said. "I am the judge and the executioner. You are the jury. You must debate with yourself about these facts. I walk out of here with the film, and you walk out alive. If I kill the girl while you try and make up your mind, then I will have to kill you, too, or you will track me down until your dying day. And I don't want to go through life wondering if you are waiting for me around the next corner."

Liese paused a moment.

She knew Lincoln was weighing the facts.

The truths.

And the consequences.

"There is a chance that you will kill me in the process," Liese said matter-of-factly. "I know your kind, Lincoln. You are not simply some messenger or delivery boy. You have been trained to pull the trigger and keep pulling it until you have no breath left in your lungs. But by then, the girl will be dead. And what happens to those who hires us to do what they are afraid to do? The film remains where you have hidden it. So it is lost for eternity. No one ever sees the pictures. My side wins by default. Your side loses."

"But their lives go on."

"And ours don't." Liese's smile was barely visible in the dim light. A soft snow was coming down through the roof and falling at her feet. "It's quite simple, Mister Lincoln. You hold our fate in your hands. We can fight it out. Or we can go home. It is a decision you have to make."

Ambrose Lincoln looked away, and his eyes swept over the burnt-out ruins of the studio. Rachel played in these rooms as a child. She had climbed up and down those stairs far too many times to count. She had worked diligently in the darkroom, processing film and making glossy prints for her father.

All of her memories were locked inside these walls.

It would not be a good place for her to die.

Lincoln did not know if he could trust Liese.

He doubted it.

Regardless of his decision, he knew he would one day regret it.

He took a long breath.

"The bricks," he said.

"What about them?"

"Check out the bricks above the counter," he said. "Eight bricks from the top, six bricks to the right. Remove the brick, and you will find the film."

Liese laughed.

He had not trusted her.

She certainly did not trust him.

"You do it," she said. "Your hands are free. Mine aren't."

Lincoln shrugged. He methodically counted down from the top and to the right. He pulled the brick out of place. Stacked behind it were five rolls of film.

How many had died for five rolls of film?

How many more would die because of them?

Lincoln turned and held them out for her.

"Leave them on the counter," she said

He nodded.

"And place your pistol beside them."

He did as he was told.

"That's not all," she said.

Lincoln stared at her.

"Now remove the Luger from your boot and pitch it toward me."

Lincoln hesitated.

"I'm sorry," Liese said. "But you would not come here with a single weapon. You have no place else to hide it but in the boot. At the moment, the Browning HP gives me leverage. The Luger would make us even. I can't take the risk."

Reluctantly, Lincoln removed the Luger from his left boot and gently tossed it to her feet.

He was at Liese's mercy now.

He knew it.

So did she.

Liese turned loose of Rachel's hair, and the girl crumpled on the floor. Liese picked up the pistols and the film, dropping them into her coat pocket.

She smiled and walked to Lincoln. She placed the barrel of the pistol under his chin, reached up and kissed his cheek.

"It was the right choice," she said. "But I have one question."

"What's that?"

"Would you have given up the film for me?"

Liese did not wait for an answer. She raced down the stairs, taking two steps at a time.

Lincoln did not move until he could no longer hear her boots running in the crust of the snow.

55.

ATTICUS CHANDLER HAD spent the last hour with the President in a small anteroom where total privacy could be guaranteed. He had long served as an unofficial, unpaid member of Roosevelt's unofficial, unpaid cabinet. And it had always been an understanding that the President preferred not being seen in public with a man who did not mind doing the dirty work of whoever was willing to pay his large monthly stipend.

Atticus moved freely within the business community across the country and throughout the world, keeping his finger on the pulse of what was good and bad for America, legal or otherwise. The President trusted him implicitly.

Atticus Chandler always had inside information that others would pay dearly to know and perhaps kill to own. Atticus brokered deals that rescued companies and bankrupted nations. He had no conscience and, at times, was rather proud of the fact that he possessed no sentimentality toward his wins or his losses.

Their mid-morning breakfast discussion, always off the record and away from the prying eyes of the press, had dealt primarily with the growing unrest in Europe.

"What's going on in Germany?" Roosevelt had asked the moment he sat down. He had no time for pleasantries.

"Germany has reinvented itself," Atticus said. "Along with Great Britain, it holds the power in Europe, and there are those who believe that the Brits have fallen a notch or two below the Germans."

"We should never have taken the heel of our boot off Germany's throat," Roosevelt said.

"I must disagree," Atticus said.

"I'm sure you have your reasons."

"Germany is a great, industrial nation," Atticus said. He leaned back and finished the coffee in his cup. "But do you know what has made Germany so great?"

"You tell me."

"America has made them that way." Atticus smiled. "Germany understands business, particularly the industrial and manufacturing side," he said. "But it is our country that sells them the technology and the raw materials to keep their factories running around the clock. Quite frankly, Germany needs us."

"And, financially, we need Germany."

"Our economy is certainly much stronger than it was," Atticus said, "and a lot of our money is new-found money because of our growing exports to Germany."

Roosevelt stared out the window for a moment. The lawn of the White House was sprinkled with snow. He looked at the darkening sky and figured rain would wash it all way before night. His mood was just as dark.

"I fear we may have to fight them again."

"Their war is not our war," Atticus said.

"I don't trust their strange and bitter little man in Berlin," the President said.

"Hitler?"

"He appears to be a warmonger."

Atticus shrugged. "Maybe," he answered. "But Hitler is not a threat to us."

"There are a lot of people who tell me otherwise."

"They are afraid of what they don't know."

"Tell me, Atticus, do they have a reason to be afraid?"

A soft knock on the door stopped their conversation. The president's receptionist opened the door and walked in. "I apologize for the interruption," she said. "But a telegram has just arrived for Mister Chandler. It was marked urgent. I hope you forgive me."

"You did right, Agnes," Roosevelt said.

Atticus smiled and took the telegram.

He slowly opened it and read: We have the film. Stop. The rolls are on their way to you. Stop. Await further instructions. Stop.

"I hope the news isn't bad, Atticus," the President said.

"On the contrary," Atticus said.

He smiled broadly, folded the telegram, and slipped it in the breast pocket of his suit coat.

He looked up, faced Roosevelt, and said with a stone face, "Your friends have absolutely nothing to be afraid of in Germany."

"How about the Jewish problem?"

"It is their problem," Atticus said.

"The Jews can't stand up to a power such as Germany."

"The Jews won't stand up."

"It's wrong," Roosevelt said.

"There is a lot in this world that is wrong," Atticus said. "We can't fix a perfect world that works for everyone."

"I have been asked to join a block of nations that are committed to stopping Hitler," Roosevelt said. "He is already threatening to move on Czechoslovakia and Poland."

"Are you?"

"No," the President said. He thought for a moment, then added, "We will support those nations. We will sell them supplies and munitions, and even planes or weapons if necessary. But I feel much as you do, Atticus."

"How is that?"

"Their war is not our war." Roosevelt. "I will not send American boys into harm's way because there are students protesting in the streets and breaking out a few windows."

Atticus left the President's office feeling as good as he had in a long time.

His people had the film.

Soon he would possess the film.

Rudolph Hinkel had been right. The hundred thousand dollars it cost him to acquire the film was pocket change.

He had a contract to sign with a German company as soon as he returned to his office. By the end of the day, if his math was correct, and, if nothing else, he did know how to exchange currency, he would be right at four million dollars richer than he had been when the first snowflakes fell that morning.

He wished he had some breadcrumbs in his pockets. He might even be tempted to go down to the marina and feed the pigeons.

56.

FOR THE PAST hour, Rachel Gruner had sat alone in the charred ruins of her father's studio. She was inside and protected from the wind, but the damp cold had managed to penetrate the cracks in the walls. Patches of snow were clustered on the floor beside her where flakes had fallen through the ragged holes in the roof. It had been home, and now it was dark and desolate. All life and signs of life had vanished on the night the glass broke.

Ambrose Lincoln had deserted her.

She had no idea where he had gone.

He said he would be back.

But when?

Or had he lied?

He had needed her because she knew where the film was hidden.

Now the film was gone.

He did not need her anymore.

Lincoln had loved her.

He had been kind and tender.

He said he would never leave her.

But for men like Ambrose Lincoln, whoever he was and whatever he did, the art of lying was as easy as breathing. After a while, they did not recognize either a lie or the truth.

Life had begun for Rachel Gruner within the walls of the studio.

It would end here.

She had no doubts about it.

Rachel heard footsteps on the staircase. She wrapped the woolen coat tighter around her shoulders, closed her eyes, and waited.

She never expected to open them again.

"The train leaves at seven thirty-eight." It was Lincoln's voice. "It will no doubt be late."

He sat down on the floor beside her.

Rachel looked up.

He was handing her a sack. "Some black bread and stew meat," he said. "It's no longer hot, but it will give you strength."

"Where are we going?" she asked.

"Strasbourg, then Katowice." Lincoln laid his head back against wall and closed his eyes. "We should get there before morning," he said. "Then again, we may not leave here before morning. No one seems to know who's in charge of the trains."

"Why are we leaving?" Rachel's voice was flat.

"This is not a safe place for you to be," Lincoln said. "There are those on the streets who want you dead."

"No one is interested in me."

Lincoln grinned. "You are the girl with the film" he said.

"Not anymore."

Rachel paused and took a bite of the bread and meat. It was cold. It was tough. She was hungry. She had forgotten how hungry she was. "You gave the film away," she said.

"It kept you alive."

"My death is nothing," she said. "People would not remember I was here or be concerned that I was gone. But the images on the film would have lived forever. They would have told the story of what happened here, the story that no one wants to hear or believe. Now others will die because the film has been destroyed. My father wanted the world to know. Now no one will know. Those who died in the streets that night died in vain."

Lincoln did not respond. He sat and watched the snow pile up on the floor. Finally he said, "We have two hours before the train leaves. You might want to get some rest if you can."

"I'm not going," she said defiantly.

"I won't leave you," he said.

"It's much easier if you go alone," she said.

Lincoln reached out and touched her hand.

He waited for her to pull it away.

She didn't.

"The film is in my boots," he said.

Rachel snapped her head around.

"Did you find the girl?" she said.

"No."

"How did you get them back?"

"I never lost them."

Rachel was shaking her head in disbelief.

"But I saw her take them."

Lincoln smiled. "You saw her take five rolls of film."

He shrugged wearily. "Your father had many rolls of film. I simply picked up five, put them in a hiding place, and made sure she found them."

"How did you know she would be here?"

"After a while, you just know."

He took a bite of his own black bread. "After a while you learn to read the shadows."

"When will the girl know she has been tricked?"

"She won't." Lincoln said. "But I fear that whoever bought the film will know what's on it before we can get out of Baden-Baden. He won't be pleased. For him, it will be a two-grave night."

"What will happen?"

"Liese will deliver the film," Lincoln answered. "She will collect her money. She will be executed before she can spend it."

"And you simply let her walk into a trap that will kill her."

Lincoln shrugged again. "It is the game we play," he said.

"What about us?"

"We have little control over what happens to us."

"Who does?"

"The engineer," Lincoln said, "and I'm hoping he won't know we're on the train."

"Do you have the tickets?"

Lincoln laughed softly. "A rich man's tickets are a poor man's death warrant," he said. He heard the words coming from somewhere beyond the depths of a distant past.

And the voice was harsh.

And bitter.

57.

AMBROSE LINCOLN HELD Rachel's arm tightly and kept her in the shadows, close to the storefronts, away from the scattered street lamps as they walked down the empty side of the sidewalk that that led toward the railroad station. German sentries were congregating outside the front door of a pub, talking loudly, laughing madly, and drinking their beer to insulate themselves from the winter cold. The snow was no longer falling, but the sky remained as black as the inside of a dead priest's confessional.

An old man sat sleeping against the corner of a building, an uneaten sandwich rotting on his lap. He had the smell of cheap whiskey on his breath.

Rachel started to speak, but Lincoln shook his head.

"Not now," he whispered.

Old men had big ears. Old men who appeared to be sleeping were not always sleeping. And drunks too often weren't drunk.

Lincoln knew but did not know how or why he knew.

He suddenly turned into the shadows of an alleyway that ran behind a row of abandoned warehouses. In the near distance, the lonely whistle of a slow-moving train broke the stillness of the night.

Beyond them, beyond the edge of the last warehouse, a maze of tracks crisscrossed their way through the yard, all leading to the train that would carry them away from the death and dying of Baden-Baden.

Lincoln stopped and pointed toward the train on track nine. Already smoke was pouring from its stack, a white thick cloud boiling up to corrupt the black sky.

"It looks like it's leaving on time," he said.

"How will we get on board?" Rachel asked.

"The baggage car."

Rachel had never seen his face as solemn, his eyes as hard.

"How do we get in?" she asked.

"I paid the porter to leave the door cracked."

"Do you trust him?"

"No."

He shrugged. "A German may have paid him more to lock it."

"But we are going anyway."

"We have little choice," Lincoln said. "The guards at the ticket windows have copies of your picture. You were in high school, maybe, when it was taken. The photograph is several years old. But you will be easily recognized."

"And you?"

"A man without a face."

"A ghost?"

Lincoln frowned. "I prefer it that way," he said.

Lincoln waited until he saw a crowd beginning to congregate alongside the track. Soldiers. Businessmen. Students. Wives. All going somewhere. All of them no doubt coming back. Only he and Rachel were leaving for good.

"There is a chance we might become separated," Lincoln said.

Rachel shuddered.

She was freezing beneath the woolen coat, but a clammy sweat had plastered her hair to her face. Her face was pallid, stripped of all makeup, and the woolen cap was pulled low over the apprehension in her eyes.

"The Germans have no respect for a Jewish girl," he said. "A select few are looking for you because they know you have the film they want to destroy. The others are little more than scavengers and vultures. To them, you are simply young and pretty. They will play with you and then kill you or lock you away for another day. The life you know will be over."

Lincoln removed the Heckler and Koch semi-automatic pistol from his belt and placed it in the palm of her hand.

Rachel stared at the pistol.

Her hand trembled.

"I can't kill anyone," she said. "Not even a German."

"I'm not asking you to kill a German."

Rachel stared at him.

"You must remember this as surely as if it were written in the Torah," Lincoln told her.

"What is that important?"

"One bullet has your name on it," he said. "If you need the pistol, use it quick and use it wisely. Death is preferable to a German soldier or a German jail."

"I could never do that," Rachel said.

"You never know what you can do or can't do until you have to do it," Lincoln said.

The pistol had grown cold in her hand.

"How many bullets does it have?" Rachel asked.

"It doesn't matter."

"Why not?"

"You only care about one bullet."

"You are asking me to be my own executioner."

"No," said Lincoln. "I'm only giving you a choice."

Lincoln moved into the crowd, taking Rachel with him and moving back toward the rear of the train. The hissing of steam grew louder as the fire roared angrily in the boiler.

A German soldier stepped down from the engine. His face was caught in the red glow of the blaze behind him, glazed with sweat, blackened with smoke.

His eyes were grim and his gaze was sweeping slowly from face to face. Occasionally he glanced down at the photograph in his hand.

Ambrose Lincoln walked up to him, his arm around Rachel.

They were the portrait of a businessman and his wife, dressed in fine woolen coats, perhaps on their way to a holiday.

Lincoln smiled.

The soldier frowned.

"What seems to be the trouble?" Lincoln asked in perfect German.

"No trouble."

The soldier looked down at Rachel, but all he saw was the top of her woolen cap.

"If I can be of any assistance, please call on me," Lincoln said.

The soldier abruptly and angrily turned around, spit once in the snow, rearranged the rifle on his shoulder, and made his way through the crowd and toward the ticket window.

The train was beginning to ease out of the station by the time Lincoln and Rachel reached the baggage car.

Lincoln looked up and down the track.

No one was in sight.

The door was cracked open.

Running alongside the train, he picked Rachel up and wedged her through the narrow opening, then climbed in behind her. The car was in total disarray, piled high with crates and cartons that had been carelessly thrown inside and hopelessly crammed together.

Rachel began to burrow her way through the jumbled accumulation of boxes to make herself a hiding place in the darkness, curled up in a space barely wide enough for her to breathe. The dust was stifling, and her legs were twisted oddly and awkwardly beneath her. The stained, rusting walls – ominous and barely visible – began to close in around her.

Ambrose Lincoln leaned against the window, watching the empty streets of Baden-Baden slip past.

The metal door slammed shut.

Rachel flinched and tightened her grip on the pistol.

The train jerked forward and gradually picked up speed as it rumbled into the mountains and toward morning. They had left the death and dying behind them, Lincoln knew. The death and dying waited for them in another time and place. It was all that had ever been promised to man.

58.

THE TRAIN WAS two hours out of Strasbourg, moving laboriously through the snow-covered countryside. The moon broke out of the heavy clouds, but only for a brief moment before being devoured again by the night. Ambrose Lincoln glanced down at Rachel as she slept amidst the boxes. She was lying next to a wooden coffin. It was empty. He wondered if it had been built for him. Lincoln removed his jacket and covered the girl against the cold air blowing past the cracks in the doors and the window.

He stared out at the tracks and felt the energy begin to drain from his muscles. For the moment, he and Rachel were hidden. For the moment, they were safe. The stop in Strasbourg had been unusually short. No passengers. No luggage. No one looking for them. No one finding them. No one with a sound mind was catching a train to Katowice in the dark, desperate hours before dawn. Soon, they would be crossing the Polish border.

Lincoln had taken the time to send a one-word telegram from Baden-Baden.

Bird.

It had been sent to a planetarium in upstate New York.

The operator had stared at him strangely but asked no questions.

Lincoln wondered if the message had gotten through, or if it had even left Baden-Baden. He feared the piece of paper still lay on the telegraph office floor or, worse still, in the hands of some German officer.

What did it mean?

The cryptographers could spend days on it.

What could it mean?

Only two people knew.

And one was on the train, riding a baggage car to Katowice.

The train abruptly and rapidly began to lose speed. Lincoln could hear the sound of the wheels grinding and groaning and complaining as they strained against the rails. He raised the window, leaned out of the car, and looked down the track.

"What's wrong?" Rachel asked.

She was on her feet now.

"Soldiers." He paused, then added, "Only two of them."

And one was waving for the train to stop.

"Is anything wrong?" Rachel asked.

"We'll find out."

The wheels kept squealing with sparks fluttering above the rails and sliding to a stop. The air outside was thick with smoke that burned in Lincoln's nostrils.

He heard the voices faintly.

"You have no right to stop this train," the engineer yelled with indignation.

The soldier pointed to the insignia on his collar. "This gives me all of the authority I need," he said.

"It's against the law."

"The Reich makes its own laws."

The door to the baggage car was jerked open, and Lincoln stared into the cold, black eyes of a captain in the German army, standing not more than six feet away. The officer blinked, unaccustomed to the darkness that surrounded the interior of the car.

Rachel crouched low, not daring to breathe.

As the officer began shoving the boxes aside, he suddenly noticed Ambrose Lincoln seated in a chair beside the window, a woolen hat pushed back on his head, calmly chewing the end of a cigar.

The officer jumped back, startled. He swung his submachine gun to eye level and demanded, "Who are you?"

"You should know," Lincoln said.

"Why?"

"The Reich put me here."

"Why would they do that?"

"To make sure no one steals anything."

He glanced toward the engineer, whose face had grown pale. His shoulders were shivering, maybe from the cold, maybe from bad nerves. Lincoln did not know for sure. He smiled and nodded.

The officer stepped back. Snow was beginning to fall around his shoulders. He had not expected to find anyone in the baggage car. He was not quite sure what to do next.

"There's nothing of value in here," Lincoln told him, yawning. "The boxes are filled with parts for your factories. The luggage belongs to poor farmers, and all they have are ragged clothes. You have no use for them. They wouldn't even make a fire hot enough to warm your hands on a cold night."

Lincoln smiled apologetically. His hand tightened on the Luger, lying in his lap, covered by an old blanket.

The officer frowned.

"Of course, there is a wooden coffin in here," Lincoln said. "But I'm afraid none of you have any need for that. Not yet anyway." He grinned sardonically.

The officer spit in disgust.

"You'd be better off with a carton of cigarettes," Lincoln said.

The German raised an eyebrow.

"And maybe a bottle of American whiskey."

"You are trying to bribe us," the officer said. It was an accusation.

Lincoln shrugged. "You have to take the good times where you find them, and there aren't many places to find them, I'm afraid. A few cigarettes … a little whiskey … it's the least I can do to help you endure the cold night."

"Where did you get them?"

"The black market in Baden-Baden." Lincoln reached into his shirt pocket and pulled out a crumpled pack of old cigarettes, offering one to the officer. "I'm sure you are no stranger to the black market."

The German grabbed the whole pack, stared at it for a moment, and quickly stuffed it into his jacket. "Where are the rest?" he asked.

The officer climbed into the baggage car with his submachine gun cradled in his arm.

Rachel was so close to him she could hear his breathing, smell the stench of his unwashed uniform. Her throat was dry, and she gripped the pistol, holding it close to her face. Now she knew what to do with the last bullet.

The moon broke free, and a shaft of light cut through the window and across Rachel's hair, ruffled by the night winds.

The officer's shoulders grew rigid. "Who is the girl?" he asked, his voice louder than before.

Lincoln kept smiling. He didn't move.

The officer grabbed her arm and roughly jerked Rachel to her feet. His eyes peeled away her clothes and lusted after every inch of her body.

"So you were keeping this one for yourself," he told Lincoln.

He laughed out loud.

He was still laughing when he died.

The soldier outside fired once.

It was wild.

His finger went limp on the trigger. He had fired his last shot.

"What happens now?" the engineer asked, wringing his hands, sweating profusely.

"You will go to Katowice as you planned," Lincoln said.

"What about you and the girl?"

"We won't be here."

"I will never see you again."

Lincoln smiled. "You never saw us at all," he said.

The train left both men by the side of the track, one inside the wooden coffin, the other lying on top of it. The snow would bury them before daylight.

59.

THE TELEPHONE CALL came in the early morning hours before daylight. The urgent ones always did. Atticus Chandler lay in the darkness of his Washington townhouse, waiting to clear his head before answering it. On the fourth ring, he rolled out of bed, reached for his robe and picked up the receiver.

"Chandler," he said.

"We have processed the film," the voice said.

The line was filled with static and crackling so loud that Atticus could barely make out the words that his man in Germany was saying.

"Go on," he said.

"I've had the pictures printed."

"Are they what we feared they would be?" Atticus asked.

"No."

Silence.

Atticus stood and pulled the robe around his shoulders. A strange chill ran through his body. It had nothing to do with the weather outside.

"What do you have?" he asked at last.

"There is a photograph of a woman playing with her child on the sidewalk in front of their home," the voice said.

"Go on."

"An old man and his wife are walking into the marketplace."

Atticus' face grew as dark and somber as his mood.

He was squeezing the phone so tightly that his hand was shaking. "What else?"

"Two young boys are kicking a soccer ball in the park."

Silence again.

Atticus walked across the floor, stood in front of the window, and stared down on the street. An early glimmer of daylight creased the sky.

The snow was turning to rain.

The voice droned on. "A congregation is walking down the steps in front of the Synagogue," it said.

"That's enough," Atticus snapped.

He reached down and picked up a stale cigar from the corner table, fumbling in the pockets of his robe for a box of matches.

"We've been duped," Atticus said.

"It appears that way."

"What happened to the girl?"

"She has been dealt with."

"Did she still have the film, or did she sell it to someone else?"

"She says she didn't," the voice said, "but she lies as easily as she tells the truth."

"Did she have my money with her?"

"No."

"Did you check the bank where we wired the funds?"

"The money is not there."

Atticus laughed softly.

He didn't expect it to be.

"What about the American?" he asked.

"He has disappeared."

"And the photographer's daughter?"

"She is gone as well."

"Together?"

"Possibly."

Atticus lit the tip of his cigar and took a long draw. It burned his throat. The smoke clouded his lungs. He coughed. He was killing himself, but, at the moment, his flirtation with death was the least of his concerns.

"She should have killed them when she had the chance," Atticus said.

"I asked her about that."

"And her response."

"She said we didn't pay to have them killed."

The static crackled as though lightning had struck it, and the line went dead.

Atticus Chandler sat down and dialed a number that only three people in Washington knew. One was the President.

Someone picked up. "The time," the voice said. It sounded like a machine.

"Seven-thirty."

Both men hung up.

+++++++++++++

AMBROSE LINCOLN AND Rachel had slipped off the train as it slowed to a crawl, coming into the outskirts of Katowice. The snow bank piled alongside the tracks had broken their fall. Morning was still an hour away, but the shops were opening up as they walked briskly down the sidewalk and past the marketplace. Lincoln had stopped just long enough to pick up two loaves of baked bread and coffee.

"How far must we go?" Rachel asked.

"Only a mile or two."

"Are we going to walk?"

"If no one sees us, then no one can report us."

"You do not trust a cab driver?"

"It is not wise to trust anyone."

"You trust me," Rachel said.

"Because I can keep an eye on you," he said.

Lincoln smiled.

"Then I shall not trust you either," she said

"You are much wiser than you were yesterday," he said. "You will live much longer that way."

Ambrose Lincoln left the main highway just before it cut past the cathedral and wound its way into the city. He and Rachel were still cloaked in the darkness, the snow came up past their knees in places, and the wind was at their back. They crossed a meadow and eased back into the forest, which protected them from the falling snow.

Rachel was breathing heavily with short, rapid bursts.

"Need to rest?" he asked.

"No," she said and kept plunging forward into the darkness.

After another hundred yards, Rachel knelt in the snow, forcing cold air into her lungs. They felt as though they were ready to burst. It had been a savage hike and was beginning to take its toll. Her lips were numb, her face had lost all feeling, and small slivers of ice were collecting on her eyelashes.

"Do you know where we are going?" she asked.

"To the far side of the trees."

"How much longer?"

"Fifteen minutes. Maybe twenty."

"Who are we meeting there?"

"I don't know."

"Where is he taking us?"

"I don't know."

Rachel looked up, perplexed. "Then what do you know?"

"That it's almost over."

In the distance, he heard the faint sounds of the plane coming out of the east. It was growing louder by the moment, banking down out of the clouds and along the tops of the trees. By the time he and Rachel reached the clearing, the big Boeing 314 was bouncing along the airstrip and slowly rolling to a stop.

The captain met them at the steps. "This is a first," he said.

"How's that?"

"The people I bring over here never come back." He paused. "What about Priestly?"

"He won't be coming back.

The captain nodded. "It figures," he said and shut the door behind them.

60.

THE BLACK LIMOUSINE sat at the far end of the runway, cloaked by the darkness of a November night. A cold rain was pounding the cement strip as the Boeing 314 bounced once, then again, and finally began straining against the wind as the captain eased back on the throttle and lost the left engine. An uneasy silence occupied the cabin. Rachel Gruner had awakened as soon as the tires ricocheted for the first time off the broken patches of pavement. She had been sleeping for the past twenty-six hours, trying to cleanse her memories of the pain and bloodshed left so far behind her. Ambrose Lincoln had not taken his eyes off the limousine, fading in and out of the plane's landing lights.

He knew that the long black car was waiting for him.

No one knew Rachel was with him.

He had left alone.

He was expected to return the same way.

The black limousine resembled a hearse in the night.

The plane rolled to a stop, and the captain climbed wearily out of the cockpit.

"This is where you people get off," he said, opening the door and lowering the steps down to the tarmac. "Your ride is already here."

Lincoln nodded, took Rachel's hand and helped her through the doorway.

"I would thank you," Lincoln said. "But I doubt if you're here."

"I'm not."

"I didn't think so," Lincoln said.

As he was walking toward the limousine, Lincoln stopped and looked back through the rain. In the doorway, he saw the small, oval face of a young woman, maybe thirty, maybe not, with long raven hair and a beauty mark or a spot of mud under her left eye. She was barely five feet tall and wore a woolen dress the color of the earth. Her skin was pale, translucent, and had not yet been touched by the sun. She was barefoot and carrying a bleached cotton sack. Her eyes were dark, filled with bitterness and regret.

She was smiling at him.

He had never seen her smile before.

Lincoln smiled and waved at her.

The captain waved back, stepped inside out of the rain, and shut the door.

By the time Lincoln and Rachel reached the limousine, the rear door was already open. They climbed inside and sat down across from a gentleman who, from the looks of his tailored dark suit and diamond cufflinks, had impeccable taste and no reason to be waiting at an abandoned airstrip for two refugees from somewhere on the other side of the world.

Lincoln had been drenched by the rains.

A dull ache had worked its way between his shoulder blades.

He hadn't eaten for almost two days.

He hadn't shaved in a week.

His shirt was torn.

His trousers were stained with blood.

His shoes were soaked.

And now he was staring down the barrel of a Walther P 38.

The big man holding the 9 mm semi-automatic pistol was smiling in a grandfatherly sort of way.

"Allow me to introduce myself," he said. "My name is Atticus Chandler." He turned to the young, broad-shouldered man beside him and shrugged. "The name of my associate is not important."

His associate had a Mauser S/42 Luger cradled in his lap.

Lincoln's gaze shifted from one man to the other.

He said nothing.

Rachel's hands were trembling.

"You are Ambrose Lincoln, I presume," the big man said.

Still nothing.

"You have something I want very badly," the big man said. "No. Let me put that another way. You have something that the President wants very badly. Let's discuss the film you have smuggled out of Baden-Baden." He shrugged again and laughed softly. "Smuggling is a very serious offense, I've been told."

Lincoln leaned back in the seat and closed his eyes.

Had it all come to this, he wondered.

The big man had made a serious mistake.

He thought all people were afraid of dying.

He did not know Ambrose Lincoln.

But Lincoln possessed a fear he had never known before.

He was afraid of Rachel dying.

+++++++++++

THE CAPTAIN OF the Boeing 314 sat slumped in his pilot's seat when he saw a black Cadillac easing out of the woods and onto the tarmac. The headlights blinked once, then again, in the gray dawn.

He sighed.

It was a long night ending.

He lowered the steps and began wearily following them to the ground.

A woman stepped out of the car. She was probably too tall and heavy for the heels on her shoes, and her suit, outlined in black, could well be gabardine. Her dark hair was cropped short and woven with a few strands of gray.

She was staring at the captain from behind thin, wire-frame glasses, which gave her the look of judicial authority. She wore little makeup, if any at all, and no lipstick. Her face was as bland as her eyes.

The rain was falling heavily around her.

She ignored it.

"You have something for me that Mister Lincoln left behind," she said.

The captain nodded, reached into his jacket pocket and removed five rolls of film. He placed them in her outstretched hands.

"He knew you wouldn't be here to pick him up," the captain said.

"Someone else wanted him worse than we did."

"And you know who it is."

"We do."

"And you let him walk into a death trap."

"The job wasn't finished."

"They'll kill him, you know."

Dr. Gretchen Sloane smiled a sad and wistful smile.

"Ambrose Lincoln died along time ago," she said.

The captain stood on the tarmac and watched the black Cadillac disappear into the gray darkness. By morning, he would be dry and Ambrose Lincoln forgotten. He had two jobs in life, and forgetting was the easiest one to remember.

61.

AMBROSE LINCOLN SAT and watched the morning find its way past the folded velvet drapes and paint the ceiling of his hotel room an off-color shade of gray. He had not moved from the sofa for three days, nor had he slept. What he feared was worse than death and just as sure.

There was a knock at the door.

He did not move.

Rachel stood and walked across the room.

"Shall I open it?" she asked.

Lincoln nodded.

Dr. Gretchen Sloane walked in, wearing a dark brown suit and heels that didn't match.

Lincoln didn't care.

He figured she didn't either.

Behind her, in the shadows, always the shadows, stood a giant of a man, wrapped in a wool overcoat and wearing a black felt Homburg pulled low to hide the scars burned on his face.

Neither spoke.

The man sat on the dark side of the room.

Dr. Sloane placed a copy of The New York Times on the table beside Lincoln. Its front page was emblazoned with four large photographs, unusual for the Times.

A young mother lay crumpled on the sidewalk. She had died trying to protect her child. The child lay beneath her. They had breathed their last together. A grinning brown shirt with a swastika sewn on the sleeve stood above them, a rifle across his shoulder.

Lincoln recognized the woman in an instant.

His heart broke, and Lincoln hadn't felt any hint of remorse or grief for a long time.

He glanced at the photograph of an old man and his wife. He was sitting with his back against a wall, his mouth gaped open, a jagged knife wound in his chest. His wife had knelt to comfort him when the bullets struck her.

Two boys were being dragged away from the park. One was one his knees, crying. The other's face had been battered. A soccer ball lay on the ground behind them.

Bodies had been stacked like cordwood on the steps of the Synagogue, and flames were erupting from the broken windows of the sanctuary.

The photographs were bold.

Vibrant.

Damaging.

The giant of a man spoke from the shadows. "The President can no longer deny what happened there," he said. "He wants to stay out of a war with Germany, and he'll stay out as long as he can. But those photographs will condemn him every day that he does. The country won't be blinded by lies or its ignorance."

Lincoln had heard the voice before.

Harsh.

And bitter.

Rachel, standing beside the window, opened the drapes, and eight floors below her, she saw two motorcycles with lights flashing escort a black hearse around the corner and down Pennsylvania Avenue.

A parade of black cars followed.

All pomp.

Mostly circumstance.

Dr. Sloane walked over to the window. "The President is not at all happy about you killing his unofficial chief of staff," she said. "He and Atticus Chandler were quite close, especially on business and foreign affairs."

Lincoln closed his eyes again and smiled.

"His death has put me in a very awkward position," the big man said.

"It's one of your choosing," Lincoln said.

"I'm not quite sure I understand."

"You knew Atticus Chandler had to be eliminated."

Silence.

"I had no idea who Atticus Chandler was," Lincoln continued, "but I knew you had decided that someone in a position of power needed to be eliminated."

Silence.

"That's why Atticus Chandler was there to meet us, and you weren't," Lincoln said.

He heard the big man sigh.

Harsh.

And bitter.

"No loose ends," Lincoln said. "There never are. Tie them up or bury them."

"But this time," the man said, "I'm afraid the President holds me responsible for your actions."

Lincoln opened one eye. It was still blurred from lack of sleep.

"Then you shouldn't worry," Lincoln said.

"Why not?"

"I didn't kill Atticus Chandler."

"He came back dead," the big man said.

Rachel looked around, her eyes flashing. "He did not deserve to live," she said softly.

Silence.

"I killed him," she said.

She looked back down at the hearse as it rolled slowly down the street beneath her. The rains had begun again. Even the November sky had worn black to his funeral.

The big man stood and began walking toward the door. "Then the execution was a just one," he said.

Ambrose Lincoln sighed heavily.

He knew the time had come.

He stood and walked to Rachel's side. He touched her arm, and she looked around at him. She smiled.

"You must go with them," Lincoln said. "They have made arrangements for you."

"But I'm staying with you."

"I'm afraid you can't."

"But you said you loved me."

"I do."

"Then you cannot send me away."

"I must."

"But why?"

Silence.

Dr. Gretchen Sloane, reached out, took Rachel's hand and led her toward the door. "Tomorrow," she whispered. "Ambrose won't be with us anymore."

+++++++++++++

HE LAY IN the darkness on a stone slab and waited.

He could already hear the footsteps coming down the hall.

He had heard them so many times before.

Ambrose Lincoln closed his eyes and focused his thoughts on Rachel. He remembered her tears, her laughter, her fears, her touch, the look of love that bathed her face in a cold, empty bedroom on the wrong side of Baden-Baden.

He remembered. He wanted to remember her forever, to hold her in his mind and never let go of the image.

But he knew that when the electrodes touched his brain, she would be gone.

Erased.

Everything would be erased.

Ambrose Lincoln had no beginning and no ending. He was always trapped and lost somewhere in between.

Alone.

The door opened, and he was moved to the gurney. The hallway grew darker. This time, he would remember, Lincoln vowed to himself. This time he would hold on to a fragment of the past.

He whispered her name.

Already the girl's face was beginning to fade.

www.ingramcontent.com/pod-product-compliance
Lightning Source LLC
Chambersburg PA
CBHW072225170626
46813CB00003B/1098